Chasing ROMEO

PO-H

Chasing ROMEO

A.J. Byrd

a
BFF
novel

KIMANI
tru
™

4-09
10-

Recycling programs
for this product may
not exist in your area.

CHASING ROMEO

ISBN-13: 978-0-373-83090-9
ISBN-10:   0-373-83090-4

© 2009 by Adrianne Byrd

www.KimaniTRU.com

Printed in U.S.A.

To my BFFs: Kathy Alba and Elliott Goins. Thanks for always having my back and keeping me grounded.

Acknowledgments

To my family and friends, thanks for all the support and love that you've given me. Again to my editor, Evette Porter, thanks for lovin' my stories and being so patient with me on this project. To my wonderful fans and readers, thank you for allowing me to do what I do. It's always a pleasure to entertain you.

I wish you all the best of love,

A.J.

A.J. Byrd, Chasing Romeo
BFF Rule #1
Always have your girl's back.

A.J. Byrd, Chasing Romeo
BFF Rule #1
Always have your girl's back.

chapter 1

Anjenai Legend—The Smart One

"ANJENAI, you better get your girl before I whup her ass!" Billie shouts, rolling her neck and planting her face dead in front of my best friend Tyler's.

I swear trouble is Tyler's shadow. We can't go anywhere without something poppin' off—and that includes just standing at the bus stop in the morning on the first day of school.

"What? Ain't nobody scared of you!" Tyler snaps back, eyes blazing up at Billie—a girl who's six inches taller and fifty pounds heavier.

"Little girl, you better get outta my face," Billie growls, slipping off her earrings.

My second best friend, Kierra, and I roll our eyes and stomp over to break it up before things get out of hand.

"Fight!" One overeager chick, watching from the sidelines, screams out causing a stampede at the bus stop this morning. Everyone picks up the chant, "Fight! Fight! Fight!"

There's no doubt in my mind that Billie can snap my girl in half without even thinking about it. She's just weighing whether giving Tyler a beat down is worth another trip to juvie.

"Come on, girl. Squash this." I clamp a hand onto Tyler's wrist and attempt to pull her away. But like always, Tyler has to put on a good show to save face.

"Get off me, Anje," Tyler shouts. "I want to hear her talk smack in my face since she's so good talking behind my back! Up here trying to say I let some boys I don't even know run a train on me!"

"Oooh," the crowd instigates.

Okay. That is foul. Billie is wrong for that. A lot of these girls get Tyler twisted because being a semi-tomboy she has a lot of guy friends. It's messed up that people think just because you hang with guys means you're doing something with them.

"Let it go," I said, mainly because I'd like our first day to be drama-free, plus I can see our bus coming up the street.

"Yeah," Kierra says, brushing her long bangs out of her eyes. "She's not worth it. Everyone knows Billie is a liar."

"Oooh," the crowd jeers.

"Who the hell you calling a liar?" Billie says as she turns her hostility toward us. "Everyone knows that the BFFs do everything together. You guys probably tag teamed up on Wayne and Freddie."

Kierra twirls around with her hands on her hips. "Ain't nobody studin' Wayne and Freddie. You're just mad cuz he dumped you cuz your kitty kat smells like fish!"

Billie swings so fast and so hard that it is amazing Kierra manages to duck the first blow. But after that, it is on. I throw my brand-new Wal-Mart book bag down and jump into the mix.

Of course, so does Billie's crew.

I feel a few punches land against my head and stomach and someone grabs a fistful of my microbraids. All in all, we hold our own—that is until the school bus arrives and our new bus driver, Mrs. Barksdale, takes over and directs the other kids to pull everyone apart.

Mrs. Barksdale still buses us to school. When we get there, Billie is taken to the school nurse and Tyler, Kierra and I end up in the principal's office. Billie's crew gets off free and clear.

Typical.

Our first day at Maynard Jackson High, a day the BFFs officially becomes high school chicks, and this is how it goes down.

So far, it looks like a repeat of junior high where the slightest thing sets Tyler off, sweet but clueless Kierra thinks she's too cute for school, and I, Anjenai Legend, worry about everything from grades to lunch money, and how to stop being such a disappointment to my granny, who's struggling to raise me and my four brothers.

I'm not doing so good in that last category.

Still, what am I supposed to do? You mess with one of us, you mess with all three of us. That's the rule. That's how it's always been. I look to my girls on my right and know that no matter what goes down, we have each other's backs. Best Friends Forever. No three words have ever been truer.

While most chicks tend to have a different BFF every other week, that nonsense doesn't go on with us. We've been inseparable since our KidsRKids Daycare Center days. I remember momma telling me stories that whenever we got together, they'd called us the giggling babies trio.

It's goofy, I know, but I don't doubt that it's true. However, our giggling days are long gone. The last fourteen years can only be best described as hell. Parents dying, parents locked up and parents who just flat-out jump ship has only strengthened our bond. Most times, it feels as if all we have are each other.

That's still two more than what a lot of people have.

The school bell rings, and I drop my head into the palm of my hands with a groan. "We're going to be late for homeroom."

Tyler just clucks her tongue and adjusts her ponytail. "Chill, Anje. It's not like it's a real class or nuthin'."

True, but Tyler is missing the point, and there's no point in me trying to explain it. Sometimes I wonder where Tyler stores all that sass and attitude. The girl is just five-foot nothing and not quite 100 pounds, but she has the thickest, shiniest hair you've ever seen on a black girl that didn't come out of a pack from the hair store. She's tomboy-cute and, like me, don't care too much for makeup and the whole nine.

Kierra, on the other hand, has bought or stole every

shade of everything from our local Rite Aid pharmacy. Words like Fuchsia Poplin, Bronze Rust and Raspberry Sugar flow out her mouth on the regular, to which Tyler and I respond with deer-caught-in-headlights stares. But I got to hand it to her, when it comes to fashion, my girl's got skillz. She can take a look, any look, out a those fancy fashion magazines and copy it—plus add her own dash of flavor—just by looking at it.

She says she going to be a big-time fashion designer one day, and I believe her.

Me? Well, I don't know what the heck I'm going to be. Right now, I just want to get through high school with as few trips to the principal's office as possible.

"Jeez. How much longer are they gonna keep us out here?" Tyler whines, glancing up at the huge black-and-white clock high on the wall next to the bell. "I don't even see how they can punish us for a fight that didn't even take place on school property," she continues to complain.

Kierra finally lifts her nose out of *Black Hair* magazine to agree. "Me, neither. I can see it if we were on the bus or something, but standing outside our apartment complex? It's bullshit."

I kind of agree and hope that our new bus driver, Ms. Tattletale, was overreaching her authority when she dragged us in here and told us to wait. We each folded our arms and waited to do battle with the powers that be, knowing full well that grown-ups like to make up rules on the fly and that we'd probably lose.

A rail-thin woman with a pixie cut emerges from

behind the long counter in front of us, standing up as she reaches for the stationary microphone and punches a button. Behind her, the intercom squawks.

"Morning students. On behalf of Principal Vincent and the teachers, I'd like to welcome you to the first day of the new school year at Maynard Jackson High School. Today's lunch special…"

I turn to my girls on my right and give them a crooked smile. It's official. We're now high schoolers.

"The last day to drop or change classes will be this Wednesday. You'll need to come to the registration desk in the principal's office…"

The door to my left busts open, and I jump in my hard plastic chair.

"In you go," a woman commands.

Three girls with identical light-skinned olive complexions and silky straight hair march into the office.

The obvious leader is tall with a fully developed body that I normally see dropping it like it's hot on those BET rap videos. Her thick, long hair is dyed a dirty, honey-blond and is iron-straight. She's pretty but wears a ton of makeup like my girl Kierra. The only flaw, in what would be considered a killer body, is her chest. It's flatter than a pancake, but that doesn't stop her swagger. She's pretty and she knows it.

The two girls trailing behind her are also video knock-outs with petite bodies (more endowed, though) and dressed in clothes that even I recognize from Kierra's latest fashion magazines.

"I wonder who they are," a breathy Kierra whispers

in my ear. I literally feel her bubbling with excitement at the possibility of making new friends.

"Who cares?" Tyler says loud enough for the mystery girls to hear.

Goldilocks cast a bored, hazel-eyed gaze in our direction and rakes us over with obvious contempt.

So much for making new friends.

Kierra jabs an elbow into Tyler's side and hisses, "Cut it out."

Blondie and her cohorts round their attention to Tyler. But before any more words are exchanged, the woman behind the registration counter turns off the intercom and interrupts us.

"Phoenix, you're in here early. I thought surely I wouldn't see you until at least first period. That's about the time your brother shows up."

As it turns out, this Phoenix even has perfect teeth, I notice, when she turns on her megawatt smile. "Hello, Ms. Callaway. It's so nice to see you, too."

Ms. Callaway's sarcastic smile vanishes from her lips. "What did they do, Nance?"

The stout woman trailing behind the girls is wearing a dark blue on light blue uniform with a butch buzz cut. Security?

"Caught 'em smoking in the girls' bathroom upstairs," the woman says, settling her hands on her hips.

"You did not!" Phoenix barks, pivoting toward the security woman with her hands on her hips. "You walked into a smoky bathroom and jumped to conclusions. You have no proof that we were the ones smoking!"

"I can smell it on you," the woman responds.

"I can smell it on you, too," the girl snaps back.

Okay, I have to hand it to her. The girl doesn't take crap off anybody.

"All right. All right," Callaway says. "Just go over there and sit down." She directs them to another row of chairs on the opposite wall from us. "Principal Vincent will see you after those girls."

The BET chicks walk to their chairs as if they were strutting down the catwalk and then sit down as if they are waiting for someone to start serving them.

I cut another glance to my girls, and we bust out laughing.

"Please, I know you hood rats ain't laughing at nobody," one chick snaps with a heavy accent. I'm guessing Puerto Rican. "Let me guess—Oak Hill housing projects. Am I right?"

Tyler is the first to jump to her feet. "Yeah, so? What of it?"

"Ladies," Ms. Callaway drones. "Sit down."

Tyler and Ms. Puerto Rico don't move. It's a stare down worthy of the record books.

"Don't try me, Raven," Callaway warns. "I'll have you in detention so fast it will make your head spin."

Raven draws a deep breath and returns to her seat. Thank goodness. Tyler would've taken the detention rather than back down. She's hardheaded like that.

Callaway fixes her eyes on Tyler and wrinkles her nose.

Raven and her friends buzz, whisper and break out in their own series of giggles.

I just roll my eyes and sigh. When the hell are we going

to see this damn principal? My butt is starting to hurt in these chairs.

"I swear these little girls today," Callaway complains, shaking her head.

"I know what you mean," Nance says. "We have more trouble out of them than the boys."

We all roll our eyes at that comment but then return to our glaring contest while we wait for our MIA principal.

Ten minutes later, the bell rings again, ending homeroom.

"Just great," I mumble under my breath, convinced that every minute that passes is confirmation of my pending expulsion.

The office door opens again, emitting the loud laughter and chatter from the crowded hallways. I don't even bother to see who's walking into the office. I'm too busy crossing my arms and moping.

Kierra bolts upright and grips my arm. "Oow!" I snatch my arm back. "What's with you?"

Kierra doesn't answer. Instead I notice her eyes have widened to twice their size and her mouth is hanging open to the point her pink Bubble Yum is noticeable in the corner of her mouth.

I look at Tyler and see her eyes glazed over as well. Finally, I turn my head to see what has transformed them into zombies only to turn into one myself.

There, standing at the registrar's desk is a tall, broad-shouldered boy with honey-brown skin, puppy-dog brown eyes and lips that you just want to rest your mouth on.

It's the first day of school, and I am in love.

chapter 2

Kierra Combs—Diva-in-training

OH—MY—DAMN! Somebody needs to bring me
a tall drink of water. I glance to my left and then to my
right and see my girls Anjenai and Tyler copping a drool
over my future boyfriend. And what's worse I see the
three fashionistas across from us also peeping and sizing
him up.

"Can I help you?" Ms. Callaway asks tall, dark and
gorgeous, while sliding on a pair of glasses and allowing
them to rest on the tip of her nose.

"Yeah, I need to change one of my classes," the mys-
terious boy says in a smooth voice that causes butterflies
to flutter in the pit of my stomach. Oh yeah. This brother
is so *mine*.

"I didn't sign up for home ec." He flashes Ms.
Callaway a half grin, and I swear to God my heart melts
clear to my toes.

"Let me see," she says, holding out her hand and then receiving what must have been his class schedule. When she turns toward a computer, Mr. Fine glances our way and unleashes his beautiful smile on us.

Be still my heart.

My future boyfriend meets my stare with the dreamiest brown eyes I've ever seen. His plump lips widen and, to cap it off, he winks.

"Which elective do you want?" Ms. Callaway asks, reclaiming his attention.

"Shop or something," he said. "I can't have my boys clown me for learning how to cook and sew." He laughs, and it's the most beautiful thing I've ever heard.

Ms. Callaway doesn't appear to be amused. "Fourth period shop is filled. The only available slot I have for Mr. Heffernan's class is seventh period, but you'll have to move your honor's English. Do you want to do that?" she asks, sliding her glasses up from the tip of her nose.

The office door opens again, and this time a small crowd of students usher inside. They all line up behind my boo. Apparently a lot of folks want to change their schedules. The last to step through the door behind them is a tall, older woman in an impeccable gray-and-white pantsuit. She has a bit of weight on her, but I can tell she knows how to make it work for her by the way she switches her hips, looking all important and stuff.

If I have to guess, I'd say she's pretty old—maybe in her mid-forties, maybe older. Sometimes it's hard to tell. Like my girl Anjenai's grandma always says: black don't crack.

"Good morning, Ms. Callaway," she says briskly as she walks behind the front desk and heads toward an office door.

Ms. Callaway glances over her shoulder. "Good morning, Principal Vincent."

I perked up. *She* is our principal? All right, girl power! I carefully take in her beaming smile and her seemingly good mood to judge whether she's the type to expel people on the first day of school.

"Good morning, Romeo," Principal Vincent says.

My boo glances up. *Romeo? His name is Romeo? I wonder if I can be his Juliet.*

"Good morning," he says warmly, and I continue to melt.

I didn't miss the principal's quick wink. What the heck is all that about? Surely she's not one of those cougar-types who prey on underage teenage boys.

Gross.

Principal Vincent's gaze swings in our direction. "Are all these ladies waiting for me?"

Callaway bobs her head while she continues to peck away on the computer. "First group toward the bulletin board were caught fighting at a school bus stop." She then nods toward the beautifully clad fashionistas across from us. "The others were caught allegedly—" she stops to make air quotes "—'smoking' in the girls' bathroom."

The principal lets out a long breath like we are the last things she feels like dealing with right now. Maybe getting expelled is in the cards.

Just great! My older sister, Deborah, is going to kick

my ass when I get home. For the past three years she has been me and my nine-year-old sister McKenya's legal guardian, even though most times she's ill-equipped for the job. It's either that or foster care. So far she's the lesser of two evils. But just barely.

"All right," she says waving for us to stand. "I'll see you young ladies first."

Anjenai is the first to jump to her feet. I'm next after cramming my magazine back into my backpack. Tyler looks as though she's preparing to remain parked in her seat.

"Come on," I hiss. "You got us into this mess."

She glares at me, but she finally climbs out of her seat. As we walk behind the registration desk, I get another peek at Romeo and mentally beg him to look up again. Unfortunately, I'm still walking and not looking where I'm going, and as a result I smack dead into the wall next to Principal Vincent's door.

"Ow!" I drop my backpack and rub my nose.

"Klutz!" Tyler laughs and then clamps a hand across her mouth.

All the kids in the office bust out laughing. I'm horrified and quickly bend down and pick up my backpack.

"Are you all right?"

I glance up, stunned to see *him* talking to me. I bite down on my gum but hit my tongue instead. "Ouch!"

Romeo lifts his eyebrows, no doubt wondering if I ride to school on the short yellow bus.

"Yeah. I'm all right." I climb back onto my feet and smile. I stand there staring, waiting. For what, I don't know.

"Will you go already?" Tyler says, shoving me toward the principal's office.

I glare at her for a second and then shift my attention back to the counter. Romeo is gone. "Thanks a lot, Tyler."

"What?"

I stomp off. Tyler's my girl and all, but sometimes she can be so clueless.

However the moment I enter the principal's office there's a drastic change in mood.

"Please shut the door behind you and then have a seat," the principal tells Tyler since she's bringing up the rear.

I sit next to Anjenai and can feel the nervousness radiate off her in waves. I completely understand. Neither one of us wants or deserves to be here.

The principal pulls out her chair and gracefully eases into it while placing her satchel on the floor. "Okay," she says, exhaling another deep breath. "Why don't we start off with your names?" She picks up a pen.

We each give our names and watch her as she writes them down.

"And who wants to go first and tell me what happened?" she asks pleasantly.

We glance at each other, but no one volunteers.

"I see." She glances at her watch. "Then maybe I should expel the three of you and be done with it. Is that what you want?"

We shake our heads but remain silent.

"All right." The principal places her pen down and leans

back in her chair to take her time to look each of us in the eyes. "Why don't we start by telling me who threw the first punch?"

That was easy. "Billie!" we answer simultaneously.

"And who is this Billie?" she asks, picking up her pen again.

We clam up and Principal Vincent tosses down the pen and lowers her head for a quick prayer. We are trying her patience and we know it, but suddenly this whole thing has the feel of being snitches. And where we come from that's one thing you just don't do.

There's a knock on the principal's door, and she commands whoever it is to "come in," without looking up.

When the door opens, a tall black man in an impeccable brown suit enters. I give him a careful once-over, and I'm more than impressed with his dark Hollywood good looks and pro athlete physique for a man of his age—probably late forties.

"Yes, Mr. Palmer?" Principal Vincent says. I notice how she straightens up in her seat and how her tone changes. If I didn't know any better, I'd think she has the hots for this Palmer dude.

"Morning, Ms. Vincent. I just came from the nurse's office. We're contacting a student's parents," he glanced down at his notepad. "A Ms. Wilhelmina Grant. They are going to need to come and take her to the hospital. Apparently she got into some scuffle, and the nurse has determined that her nose is broken."

Anjenai groans while Tyler's face lights up. My girls' reactions don't go unnoticed by the principal.

"I take it that this is our Billie?"

Palmer glances up at us. His eyes are so dark they're almost hypnotizing. I could see why older chicks would be into him. Heck, if I was a little older... Nah. I'll take my hottie Romeo any day of the week.

Palmer's interest in us perks up. "Are they Jackson's newest Girls Fight Club?"

"Appears that way," the principal says, crossing her arms. "Not very talkative though. Girls, this is Vice Principal Palmer." She then went on to introduce us to him and what little she knew of our situation.

"I don't see how you can punish us for something that happened off school property!" Tyler finally snaps. She's probably tired of sitting up in this office.

I know I am.

Palmer's brows shoot up. I can't tell whether he's annoyed or amused by Tyler's smart mouth. I'm a little annoyed myself even though I know Tyler's need to fight all the time has a lot to do with her mother walking out on her and her dad a couple of years ago. I know she has a lot to work out of her system, but damn. She needs to learn to let stuff go every once in a while.

Her point is worth taking into consideration. However, Principal Vincent argues that the bus stop is an extension of school property.

Since when?

In the end we wind up with Saturday detention and a promised call to our parents or guardians.

Great. I can hardly wait to hear my sister's mouth.

chapter 3

Tyler Jamison—Tough Chick

I hate Principal Vincent.

I hate this school.

I hate my life.

The only thing good about this day is that I broke Billie's nose for talking smack behind my back. At least now people will know that *this* new girl is not to be messed with.

Me and the BFFs.

It's bad enough the Atlanta school board rezoned everything so instead of attending Riverwood High, like we've been planning since the first grade, we now had to come to this boring-ass middle of the road suburban b.s.

Everybody knows the black kids up in this school are nothing but a bunch of sellouts: walking white, talking white and looking white—like those three girls outside the principal's office, Phoenix and 'em. The kids over at Riverwood keep it real.

Here, ain't nobody bumping music in the hallways or working out to the latest dance moves. All I see is busy-bodies texting on cell phones and jocks actin' like they rule the world or something.

By the time I hike my way clear across school for my first period American history class, there's just fifteen minutes left.

"Surely, you're not just *now* coming into my class?" Mr. Carson, a nerdy, pencil-thin white man asks from behind his desk when I approach.

I just shrug. "Better late than never they say."

A few kids in earshot laugh.

Mr. Carson doesn't. Instead, he just snatches the hall pass from my hand and glances at it. "Ah, coming from the principal's office. Just lovely. Another troublemaker. Why am I not surprised?"

"I don't know. Why aren't you?"

More laughter.

Mr. Carson's eyes narrow. "Watch yourself, young lady." He holds my bored gaze a few seconds and then turns to the stack of books behind him and hands me one. "I have assigned seating in this class," he tells me, opening a black folder. "You're sitting in the empty desk in the third row behind Ms. Dix. Ms. Dix, can you please raise your hand?"

One hand shoots up. Einstein fails to also mention that desk behind Ms. Dix is the only empty one available. I didn't need the visual aid.

As I march to my chair, Mr. Carson tells me the assignment is on the board. Read chapter one, and do the review questions at the end.

I just plop into my seat and cross my arms.

I don't feel like reading.

The girl in front of me, a high yellow girl with bright shiny eyes and cheeks so round they look like the size of plums, swivels around in her chair. "Did you get in trouble in the principal's office?" she whispers.

I shrug. "Kind of."

"What did you do?"

"Broke a girl's nose," I boast, puffing out my chest.

Instead of turning and cowering away, like I hoped she'd do, the girl's glossy lips just drop and her eyes brighten. "Don't tell me you're the girl who broke Billie Grant's nose."

Good. The news travels fast around here. "She had it coming."

"Hell yeah she did." She leans forward. "I'm Nicole and now one of your biggest fans."

Huh? I never had a fan before.

"Ms. Dix, please turn back around in your seat," Carson snaps.

Nicole rolls her eyes and swivels back to face the front of the class but not two minutes later she turns again and whispers. "Looks like you might have another fan."

I frown. "Who?"

She nods her head, and my gaze follows her lead two rows over. It's that cute boy from the principal's office Anjenai and Kierra were drooling over. Our eyes connect for just a second before another boy whispers something and draws his attention.

I blink and turn my head. Damn, he *is* sort of good

looking. But with the long lashes, he may be just a little too pretty boyish for me.

Maybe.

"Oooh. You better not let Phoenix Wilder hear about this."

I have an instant recall of the name. Surely there aren't two chicks here with that ridiculous name.

"Phoenix?"

The class bell rings.

Everyone jumps out of their seats like toasted Pop-Tarts in a rush to leave Mr. Carson's boring ass class.

"Don't forget to read chapter two tonight," he yells above the exiting herd. "There will be a quiz tomorrow."

"Damn. They sure don't waste time passing out homework."

"Well, what do you expect?" Nicole says smiling. "We're high school students now."

Is this chick always this damn happy? I grab my backpack and turn from my desk only to crash into a large chest that smells so divine it makes my knees weak. "Hey, watch where you're going," I yell, quickly recovering.

"You were the one walking," the boy says with an infectious laugh.

I glance up to see it's that boy from the principal's office again.

"Hi, Romeo," Nicole says dreamily beside him.

"Oh, hey." He spares her a brief glance and then turns his attention back to me. "Hey, is it true you're the one that broke Billie Grant's nose?"

"First of all, my name ain't 'hey' it's Tyler."

Two boys I hadn't noticed chuckle behind him.

"Man, I told you those girls from Oak Hill ain't no joke."

I slip my backpack over my shoulder and settle my hands on my hips. "No, we're not, so stop laughing, peanut head."

"Oooh," peanut head number two coos, covering his laughter with his hand but then quickly flashes a smile.

Despite my name-calling, the two boys are actually pretty cute. One holds a striking resemblance to the singer Chris Brown while the other could win a Bow Wow–lookalike contest if he was a few inches shorter.

"Ah, so you *are* the one," Mr. Inquisitive says. The longer he stands there, the longer that heavenly scent seduces me.

"Yeah, so what of it?" I say, wanting this conversation to hurry up and end before I turn into Kierra and start swooning at this guy's feet.

"Nothing. I just wanted to shake your hand." He offers his hand. "My older sister used to hang with Billie and got tangled up in some mess that landed her in juvie. I'm glad to see her finally get what's coming to her. Had she been a guy, me and my boys would have handled her a long time ago."

So what, he was thanking me for my services?

His hand is still suspended between us and I decide to let it hang. I didn't bust Billie's nose for him.

"I'm Romeo, by the way."

"Congratulations," I say. "Excuse me." I try to squeeze my way past him. He's wasted enough of my time.

"Oh, all right, Ms. Thang," he says with an open smile.

I stop and spear him with my best "say what?" glare.

"I mean, 'Tyler,'" he corrects himself, still smiling.

I turn and roll up out of there before those beautiful lips have me smiling back at him.

"Ohmigod," Nicole squeals, rushing up behind me. "I can't believe you just did that. Do you know who he is?"

"No and I don't care," I lie.

"Then you're the only girl in this school who doesn't. He was the biggest star on freshman varsity team last year."

Damn. That means he's a year older than me.

"Girl, you got skills. Wait until everyone hears how you dissed him like that. Every girl will think you're crazy."

"Look." I stop in the middle of the hallway. "Let's get one thing clear. I don't care what people think about me. I'm my own person, and I do what I want to do. Mr. Romeo can go take a flying leap off a tall building for all I care."

"Wow." Nicole's eyes widen. "Can we be like best friends or something?"

I frown and then laugh. "I already have two best friends. I'm not in the market for any more."

chapter 4

Romeo Blackwell—Mr. Football

okay. I've never been dissed by a girl like that in all my life. What is she—all of five-foot-nothing and packing more attitude than her body can handle? Shoot. Half the girls in this school fall all over themselves if I just say "hi" to them, but she acted as if I was bothering her.

My boys Chris and Shadiq razzed me quite a bit after Tyler left me standing like a fool in Mr. Carson's class.

"Hey, maybe we need to stop by the boys' room so you can wash the rest of that egg off your face," Shadiq jokes, pounding me hard on the back.

"Very funny," I say, as I finally head out of Mr. Carson's classroom. When we pour out into the hallway, I see Tyler still talking to Nicole.

"Don't tell me you're going to go over there to crash and burn again." Chris laughs. "What? Are you a glutton for punishment today?"

"I didn't crash and burn," I say, irritated. "I wasn't trying to hit on her."

"Yeah. Whatever, man." Shadiq gives me another pound. "I gotta head out. Catch you later."

"Me, too. I have biology over in the next building. See you at lunch," Chris adds.

I nod and rush to my locker. I'm now pretty much pressed for time. This year my locker is on the first floor, and when I get there, the lock combination I was given doesn't work. After the fourth try I hit it out of frustration, and the damn thing actually pops open.

"Nice trick." I glance to my right where this cute freshman girl wearing a multicolored outfit smiles back at me. I know she's a freshman because she still has that junior-high look about her.

"Yeah. Well. I got that magic touch," I brag.

Not unusual, she laughs along with the joke. It's a little bubbly but still cute.

She opens the locker next to mine and tries to dump all the items from her backpack, but instead half of it hits the floor. That's when I recognize her. "Hey, weren't you in the principal's office this morning? The one that ran into the wall?"

Before I can get an answer, a familiar angelic voice floats over to me.

"Romeo."

I turn, and sure enough it's Phoenix and her cronies Bianca and Raven closing in on me. "Hey," I say and slam my locker door. I want to make a hasty exit, but the damn thing bounces back open.

"Why didn't you stop and talk to me in the office this morning?" she asks, pulling her innocent look and batting her eyes at me. Seriously, I'm so sick of her head games I don't know what to do.

We've been together off and on since the sixth grade. We've always been like the most popular couple in school. But I'm getting bored with our routine and her constant need to try and make me jealous. All Phoenix wants to talk about is fashion, makeup and fashion. Oh and let's not forget—who was cool and who was not. The list changes every week.

Every once in a while she'll pretend to be interested in what I want to talk about, but I always notice a bored glaze would gloss over her eyes if I say more than five sentences.

It's all about her and I'm sick of it.

"Don't tell me you're still mad at me about that little fight we had Saturday night," she says, sliding close to me—mainly for her girls' benefit.

Mercifully, the bell rings.

"I gotta go."

"Romeo," she sputters after me.

I toss a couple of deuces her way and keep it movin'. I'm late for Ms. Lopez's Spanish class, but I breathe a sigh of relief when she doesn't give me too much grief about it. So far it pays to be the rising star on campus—that and having a personal relationship with the principal. Either way I'm not going to look a gift horse in the mouth.

I chose Spanish this year as an elective because I heard how easy it is. I really need easier classes given how I barely scraped by last year. The only bummer is that I arrived too late to get a good seat in the back. I pick out the first vacancy across the room, and as I head over that way, I notice how most the girls' eyes follow me.

I play it cool—flash a couple of smiles—but then I genuinely light up when I see who's sitting in front of the empty desk and talking to a cute girl with a head full of small braids.

"Oh hey," I say.

Tyler glances up at me, looking more bored than when she left me standing in Mr. Carson's class. "We meet again."

"Lucky me."

I laugh. I really like this girl's style. Taking my seat, I immediately lean forward to whisper at her back. "Hey, what's your problem?"

She turns in her seat. "I told you before. My name ain't 'hey.' And at the moment, you're my problem."

"And earlier?"

"Again—you." She faces the front again while Ms. Lopez begins handing out books.

I'm confused. What the heck did I do to upset her so bad? I can't think of a single thing. Maybe it's true what they say: Oak Hill girls are tough as nails.

That could be a good thing.

BFF Rule #2
Never let a guy come between us.

chapter 5

Anjenai—Friendly Competition

My mouth nearly hit my desk when Tyler mouths off to that dreamy hunk Romeo. When Tyler finally glances my way again, I give her my "what-on-earth-is-wrong-with-you?" stare, and in response she just rolls her eyes and slumps down in her desk.

Okay. Tyler has definitely lost her mind.

Ms. Lopez's class seems like it's going to be an easy one. For our first day we just learn our names in Spanish and share what few Spanish words we know.

Tyler is happy to mouth off a few words and then act like she didn't know they were curse words.

The class gets a good chuckle out of it—including Romeo.

Swear to God every time he laughs my stomach quivers like it's full of butterflies. I can tell I'm not the only one. The other girls in the class are trying to break their necks to get a good look at him.

The only one who acts like they are completely unaffected by him is Tyler. Then again, maybe she's trying too hard to act like she is unimpressed.

When the bell rings, Tyler takes off so fast I have to call after her to prevent her from leaving me.

"Okay, what gives?" I ask, catching up with her.

"Nothing. I have English next, and I don't want to be late."

"What? Do I have Boo Boo the Fool written across my forehead?" I ask, trying to keep up. For a short person, she has impossibly long strides. "What's up with you dissing a guy as fine as Romeo like that?"

For an answer she just rolls her eyes.

"Look, let's just talk about it later," she says. "I'm in a hurry. My next class is in the other building."

And just like that, she takes off running. I stop and stare after her. I swear that girl is getting stranger every day.

My next class, biology, puts the *b* in boring so I occupy my time practicing writing my future boyfriend's name:

Romeo Romeo romeo

When I was through with that, I tried our names together:

Romeo & Anjenai Anjenai & Romeo Romeo luvs Anjenai

And of course my future married name:

Mrs. Romeo Blackwell Mrs. Anjenai Blackwell Mr. and Mrs. Romeo Blackwell

I smiled all the way through class. By the time the bell rings, however, I'm also starving. Maynard Jackson High's school cafeteria looks old despite the fresh coat of green paint, but it's also huge. I look around to see whether Kierra or Tyler has beat me here but then quickly grab a table to reserve seats before they are all taken.

"What do you think you're doing?" some chick hollers close to my right ear.

I jump out of my skin only to find it's that snooty chick Phoenix and her back-up divas. "I'm about to sit down," I tell her.

"Not at our table you're not."

I look at the table and then back at her. Just then Tyler and Kierra join the small circle.

Goldilocks gets bold and steps toward me.

"I don't see your name written on it," Tyler sasses.

Oh, great. Here we go again.

"It doesn't have to be. Everyone knows that this is the Red Bones' table."

Tyler plops her backpack down in one of the chairs. "Not anymore."

Me and Kierra follow suit and then cross our arms to let them know we aren't going to back down. In reality, I'm praying this won't end up being another fight. Surely expulsion will replace our Saturday detention.

While our second stare down ensues, I suddenly become very aware of how quiet the cafeteria has become. Really, you would have thought we were in the middle of a funeral.

We probably were—ours.

"Look, little girl," Phoenix sneers.

"I got your little girl," Tyler snaps, swirling her neck and settling her hands on her hips.

Yep. It's gonna be another fight.

"Ladies, is there a problem?"

None of us had to look over to recognize the security officer Nance Foster's voice. And still neither side backed down.

"Don't tell me you all are ready to get another Saturday detention," Nance inquires.

Silence.

"Phoenix?"

She grinds her teeth. "No, ma'am," Phoenix finally spits out, her eyes promising that this isn't over by a long shot.

"Good. Then find a seat."

Thrusting up her chin while her eyes still throw daggers, Phoenix jerks away and barks at her shadows. "Come on, girls. We'll take care of this later."

The moment they walk away, the cafeteria erupts with thunderous applause with a few hoots and whistles thrown in for good measure.

I turn to the crowd undoubtedly looking dazed and confused.

A few more people climb to their feet almost as if they are expecting us to take a bow. I slide into my chair with an uneasy smile, and Kierra takes the seat next to me and grabs my arm.

"I can't believe it. We're already popular on our first day!" she exclaims excitedly.

"Yeah, but for the wrong reasons," I complain, pulling out my packed lunch from my backpack: a PB&J sandwich, an apple, a handful of Cheetos and a juice box.

"Ohmigod!" A girl pops up next to Tyler. "I can't

believe what I just saw. I'm truly you girls' biggest fan."
The girl can give Kierra serious competition for the title
of Ms. Bubbly.

"I thought you were *my* fan," Tyler says with a half
laugh.

"I am!" She plops her lunch tray down and invites
herself to take a seat. "Truly."

"What—you starting a fan club?" Kierra asks Tyler.
Obviously, she's just as confused as I am.

"You guys are like rap stars now," the girl goes on.
"Before the end of the day everybody in school is going
to know you guys stood up to the Red Bones. Oh, my
name is Nicole, by the way." She waves with an even
brighter smile. Looking at her wide smile makes my own
cheeks hurt.

"I'm Anjenai," I say.

"Kierra."

"Tyler."

"Of course I know your name, silly." Nicole slaps a
hand on Tyler's shoulder.

Tyler looks at the girl's hand and then waits for her to
remove it. It's Tyler's new thing. She doesn't really care
to be touched all that much. I know because she can
barely tolerate our group hugs anymore. Her momma just
up and leaving like she did really messed her up.

"What is a red bone," I ask, the title just now hitting me.

Nicole gives a simple shrug. "It's sort of self-
explanatory, really. Look at them."

I glance up to see the Red Bones settling into a different table with their lunch trays—their gazes still blazing.

"What? You're about as light skinned as they are. Why aren't you a part of their group?"

"It's more than that. It's the whole look, money and connections."

"If they are so rich and well-connected, why aren't they going to a private school or something?" Tyler asks, continuing her combative glare from across the room.

Nicole crams some food into her mouth and keeps talking. "They used to—until they got kicked out." She leans forward and whispers, "I heard that they hazed some chick that wanted to be part of their clique. The girl got seriously hurt, and her parents sued everyone involved. The lawsuit is still going on."

"For real?" Kierra asks, wide-eyed.

I'm a little surprised myself and give the fashion divas another dagger-look.

Nicole sits up again and shrugs. "Yeah, but some people say Phoenix got kicked out because she got caught having sex with her boyfriend in her dorm room."

"Now *that* I can believe," Tyler and I say at the same time.

We glance at each other and—no kidding—I think Tyler finally graces the school with her first genuine smile of the day.

"So how long have you guys been friends?" Nicole asks.

"Forever," Kierra brags.

The three of us lean over together to flash Nicole our gold engraved necklaces.

"B-F-F," Nicole reads.

"Yep. Best friends forever." I beam at her and then glance at my girls. I'm hit with memories of giggling sleepovers, hopscotch and jacks tournaments and even lame attempts to run away from home together. We really have done it all.

We've also done a lot of crying…

"Wow. You guys are so lucky." Nicole sighs with an unmistakable note of envy. "The girls in this school are nothing but a bunch of beeyotches, and they'll stab you in the back the moment you turn around. Trust me on this."

With a snap of a finger Nicole went from being bubbly to bitter. I wonder what that's all about.

Laughter booms in the cafeteria, and we all glance up to see a swarm of good-looking guys spill inside. My gaze, of course, zeroes in on Romeo.

"Isn't he dreamy?" Kierra asks, sighing. "I'm in love, and his locker is right next to mine."

"Really?" I perk up at this news. "Well, he's in my and Tyler's Spanish class."

"He's also in our American history class," Nicole tosses in. "Isn't that right, Tyler?"

"So what?" Tyler bites into her sandwich while holding on to that aloof attitude again. The one I'm not quite buying anymore.

"Sooo," Nicole goes on, her smile returning. "He actually tried to talk to you today, and you left him standing in Mr. Carson's room with his mouth hanging open."

"Shut up!" Kierra dropped her minibag of Cool Ranch Doritos to stare at Tyler.

"You're lying," I accuse. Please, please, please God don't tell me my future husband has the hots for my best friend.

"True story, isn't it, Tyler?" Nicole asks.

Kierra and I hold our breaths.

"You know, you have a big mouth," Tyler snaps at the girl.

"What?" Nicole looks hurt.

"You like him," I say, finally putting the pieces together. Well, I'll be damned. Tyler, who has a string of male friends and who has never once liked any of them for a boyfriend, *finally* has a crush on someone?

Somebody stop the presses.

"I do not!"

I open my mouth to argue, but then Kierra grabs my arm.

"Oh snap! He's coming this way."

I glance up in time to see him and a laughing crew of boys follow him to our table.

Oh Lord, please don't let me pass out.

chapter 6

MY boo is walking straight toward me. My boo is walking straight toward me. I make a couple of quick signs-of-the-cross despite not being Catholic. Oh God, there's no time for me to check my hair and makeup before he arrives at our table.

"Hey, aren't you girls at the wrong table?"

I sigh and close my eyes. "Oh, that golden voice." Someone kicked me. "Ouch."

The guys snicker, and it hits me that I said that out loud. I open my eyes to see Romeo staring dead at me.

"Thanks," Romeo says. "I think."

My face is on fire. What I wouldn't give to be able to shrink down to about two inches right now.

"This is the Red Bones' table," one of the guys informs us, reaching over and grabbing one of Anjenai's apple slices. He's a nice-looking hottie, too, but he has nothing on my boo.

"Hey!" Anjenai pops him on the back of the hand. "Go get your own food."

"Chill out, Chris," Romeo tells him.

"What? It is."

"Not anymore." Tyler crosses her arms. "This table is public property."

Oh God, please tell me she doesn't expect us to fight the boys, too. We seriously need to have a "come-to-Jesus meeting" real soon. I'm a lover...not a fighter.

"Let me guess," Romeo says, smiling down at Tyler. TYLER??!!!

"You chased the Red Bones off as well."

"We all did," I jump in. Love my girl, but I'll be damned if I'll let her get all the glory on this one—especially when it seems to impress my boo.

One side of Tyler's lips kick up. "Yeah. My girls always have my back."

"Damn right." I thrust up my chin.

The group of boys behind Romeo laughs.

"Hey, y'all," Chris says, looking at me. "Check out Mighty Mouse over there. What did you do, kick out someone's ankles?"

"Hey! Who are you calling Mighty Mouse, peanut head?" I snap back in response.

The boys' laughter is like a sonic boom.

"That's the second time today someone called you that!" His friend to his right slaps him on the back. "That makes it official, Shadiq."

Shadiq, with his fine Bow Wow-looking self, glares at me. "Like I care what some pip-squeak, Wal-Mart-shopping hood rat says about me!"

Tears leap into my eyes. I didn't buy this outfit at Wal-Mart.

Tyler jumps to her feet and pushes Shadiq back. "What the hell is your problem?"

"Ooh." The circle of boys around them cracks up.

"What—you like picking on girls?" Tyler challenges.

Shadiq stares back at Tyler in shock.

Romeo jumps in between them. "Whoa. Whoa. Whoa. Everybody calm down."

"Whatever. You better check your boy," Tyler warns.

"Romeo, what are you doing over here?" Phoenix's syrupy voice slips in a second before she pushes her way to his side. "We're sitting at another table today," she says as if the choice had been hers to make. "Come on, I saved you a seat, baby."

Baby????

Romeo looks hesitant to go.

"Cool," Shadiq says, his eagerness to leave this sticky situation evident on his face. I can't say I hate to see him ago.

"Check you later," Romeo says to our table and then allows his *girlfriend* to lead him away.

"Are you okay?" Anjenai asks leaning toward me.

"Yeah," I mumble. "He's an ass."

Tyler plops back down into her seat. "I hate this school."

"I should have known *she* would have sunk her claws into the finest boy in the school."

"They've been dating like forever," Nicole shares and

then leans forward. "Romeo was the one she'd snuck into her school dorm."

My heart sinks even further. "Do you think they're—" I lower my voice "—having *sex?*"

"If you were dating him, wouldn't you?" Nicole tosses back at me.

I glance over my shoulder and back at the Red Bones' new table and soak in Romeo's fine profile. "Dang, I would do anything to be his girlfriend."

"Yeah, me too," Anjenai adds. "'Course I'd settle for him noticing I'm alive first."

Something about the Red Bones' loud laughter and open glances toward our table tells me we're the topic of the conversation. "Maybe it wasn't such a good idea to get on those girls' bad side," I say.

Nicole sneers, "Oh, please. Phoenix is such a fake. She keeps her friends close and her enemies closer. Half the time I can't tell which Bianca and Raven are. Look at her."

I am looking. Her new seat at the moment is Romeo's lap, and he doesn't seem to mind. Bianca and Raven are flirting with his two main sidekicks Chris and Shadiq.

"She's pouring it on thick to win Romeo back," Nicole says.

Anjenai and I twirl back in our seat at that. "Get him back?"

Nicole bobs her head and shoves the last of her spaghetti into her mouth. "They broke up a couple of weeks ago. I hope for good this time. He deserves so much better than her."

"How is it that you know all this stuff?" Tyler asks.

"Easy." Nicole shrugs. "Phoenix is my half sister."

We look at each other. That certainly sheds new light on the situation. Before I know it, I'm pumpin' our fourth wheel for as much information as I can get. Apparently, she and Phoenix have the same father but different mothers. Phoenix's mother being his wife and Nicole's mom not. They were literally brought up on opposite sides of the tracks.

Phoenix's rich.

Nicole not so much.

This past summer, after her father's insistence, Nicole was subjected to staying with him and her half sister. According to her, it was one of the worst summers of her life. The Red Bones did nothing but pick on her and talk about her *cheap* clothes and size 14 body.

By the time lunch was over with, I couldn't believe I'd ever admired Phoenix and her friends.

"Well, you're more than welcome to hang out with us at our table," Anjenai tells her as we head out of the cafeteria.

"Yeah. Anytime," I cosign.

When Tyler doesn't say anything, I glance over and catch her watching Romeo and Phoenix as they continue to laugh and smile at each other.

I can't believe it. It's the first time in history that Tyler actually likes a boy—my boy.

Not good.

"I'll catch you guys later," I tell them and rush off to my locker, thinking. If what Nicole shared with us is true then that means Romeo is technically available.

I stop by a downstairs bathroom and refresh my makeup. But looking at the image staring back at me, my spirits plummet. While I tend to think of myself as pretty, I'm nowhere as beautiful as Phoenix or any of her cronies.

How on earth am I going to steal someone like Romeo away from her? I shake my head and rush to my locker. I'm there two seconds before Romeo shows up. He hits the metal door and like before it pops open.

Don't look at him. Don't look at him.

I open my locker.

"Hey, um, what my boy said—"

I glance over stunned to see him actually talking to me again.

"—he didn't mean anything about it," he says. "Shadiq was just playing around. He can be a real ass sometimes."

Breathe. Breathe. Oh-MY-GOD!

He sort of ducks his head. "So are we cool?"

He's talking to me. Say something. "Um, yeah. I was thinking about getting rid of these old clothes anyway." What in the hell did I say that for? I just made this outfit a couple weeks ago.

Romeo looks me over. "I think you look cute."

OH-MY-GOD! Breathe. Breathe. "Thank you," I manage to say.

He winks, closes his locker and strolls off.

I watch him melt into the crowd with a secret smile. "He is sooo gonna be mine."

chapter 7

Tyler—Hoop Dreams

wouldn't you know it. Anjenai and I end up in gym class with the Red Bones. Even though I can hear them buzzing and snickering behind our backs, this time I change up my game and decide to ignore them.

Anjenai, on the other hand, looks like she's more bothered by their cattiness than I am for a change. I know this isn't how she envisioned our first day at high school. I feel bad about that because it is sort of my fault.

Me and my temper.

I attempt to apologize, but she just waves it off and flashes me a smile.

"Don't worry about it," she says. "We'll make lemonade out of lemons."

I smile and appreciate her trying to make me feel better about the situation. Out of the three of us, Anje is what I'd describe as the brainy and sensitive one. She'd even turned down the opportunity to advance to the tenth grade just so she would stay in the same grade with me and Kierra.

Anjenai is cool like that.

Despite being described as a tomboy, I'm not really all that into sports. Never have been. Of course I've played the occasional hopscotch, double Dutch and even a little tetherball, I just never really cared to get all sweaty. So in gym class today Coach Whittaker gave a soul-stirring speech about the game of basketball and how close Jackson High has come to winning the championship for the past four years that I actually find myself thinking about trying out for the team.

Crazy I know.

Being the first day of school, the class didn't have to dress out. None of us had any clothes to change into. Still Coach Whittaker had racks of basketballs lined up, wanting to see how many of us could make a basket.

I'm not a complete stranger to the game. At Oak Hill, a lot of the boys in the complex play at the half court near the crappy playground, plus my dad is a college basketball junkie.

I lean over and ask Anjenai what she thought about joining, and she gives me a casual shrug that really tells me she isn't all that interested.

The court is divided in half. The girls take one side with Coach Whittaker, and the boys take the other side with Assistant Coach Smith.

We all have to participate, whether we are in sneakers

or not. The assignment is just to take turns at the free-throw line and try to make a basket.

As expected, most of the girls are pathetic.

The Red Bones must have decided to make a game of who could throw the ball nowhere near the basket the best and then collapse into a fit of giggles.

I watch Phoenix's fake smile, fake laugh and fake everything else and wonder what Romeo sees in a girl like her.

Eventually, it's my turn. I take the ball, bounce it a few times, aim and fire it off. The ball glides into the basket with a whish.

The girls clap.

"Go again," Coach Whittaker says.

I make three more baskets, and then the coach directs me to throw from the right side of the court, then the left. The left, apparently, is my weak side. All in all, I think I did all right.

"Very good," the coach says and then asks me my name.

I toss the ball to Anjenai. Honestly, I don't think that she would do much better than the other girls. I'm not dissing my girl, but I never pictured her as the athletic type either.

I squash that line of thinking the minute she makes the first basket, then the second. Soon, the coach is also repositioning her to different spots on the court.

She makes every basket.

Coach Whittaker moves her farther back. But it doesn't matter. Anjenai makes them all. Then at last, she is moved to half court.

The boys stop playing to watch as well.

Anjenai bounces the ball a couple times, her face set in heavy concentration. At last, she finally takes aim and fires off her shot.

I'm literally holding my breath as the ball flies through the air. But just like the other balls, it flies into the basket like it had a homing device.

The entire gym erupts into cheer, and everyone races to congratulate her.

If I hadn't seen it with my own eyes I wouldn't have believed it. I run out to my girl, give her a high five and then wrap my arms around her.

"Girl, where did you learn to shoot like that?" I yell above the crowd.

A smiling Anjenai shrugs. "It's just geometry."

"No. That was amazing," I shout. And it was. It was like crazy 1990 Michael Jordan stuff.

"All right, everybody. Calm down," Coach Whittaker shouts.

Anjenai and I continue to jump up and down. I'm so proud of her, I can't stand it.

"Calm down," the coach repeats.

I then notice Romeo standing in the crowd. How had I missed him in the class? One thing for sure, the admiring glint he'd shared with me earlier was now directed at Anjenai. Something kicks me in the gut.

Something like jealousy.

chapter 8

Romeo—Who's That Girl?

I have never seen a girl shoot like that in my entire life. The girl has completely blown me and my boys' minds. I *know* Coach Whittaker is gonna make sure she gets her on the girls' basketball team, for real.

One look at the coach, and I can see that she's practically salivating over the possibilities for this year's team. And I don't blame her.

"Who is she?" Chris shouts from my right.

"Looks like she's friends with that girl you were talking to earlier," Shadiq adds.

It's then I notice Tyler hugged up around the mystery girl's neck.

"Yeah. Yeah," Chris says. "She was at the lunch table, too."

I finally bob my head, remembering. I start to move through the crowd. When I get near, her eyes turn toward me, and I have to admit, the girl has a nice look about her. She seems friendly with an honest face. Her long, curly eyelashes have a way of hooding her emotions.

"Where did you learn to shoot like that?"

"It's my first time," she says.

I blink in surprise and wonder if I misread her honest face. First time? She's gotta be kidding me.

"Well, you're certainly a natural," I say. "I know I'd kill to be able to shoot like that."

"It was easy really," she admits.

"Easy?" Chris echoes close to my ear. "C'mon. The girl gotta be playin' us."

The coach finally calms the crowd. "Okay, honey, what's your name?"

"Anjenai Legend," she tells her.

I repeat the name to myself and think it does have the ring of a star athlete.

"Have you ever thought about trying out for the girls' basketball team?"

She looks toward Tyler and shrugs. "No, not really."

"Well, you definitely should," I say.

"That's right," the coach adds, trying to keep her excitement below the radar.

"I don't know." Anjenai hesitates, glancing between me and the coach before turning her attention back to Tyler. "What do you think?"

Tyler lifts her shoulders, looks at me. "I don't know. It's up to you."

Anjenai looks scared to commit to anything. "Well, to be

honest, I may be able to stand and throw, but running and throwing is another matter. I'm not all that coordinated."

"Well, that's what practice is for," Coach Whittaker says, not willing to give up on a potential star.

"Yeah, I could show you a few moves too, if you like," I offer.

She blinks up at me wide-eyed, while the base of her neck darkens as if I've embarrassed her or something.

"Really?" she asks. "You would teach me?"

I shrug. "Sure. Why not?"

Out of nowhere, Phoenix slinks to my side.

"Baby, do you think that's such a good idea?" She glances over at the girls. "Really, when do you have time to babysit a freshman?" She chuckles and then her girls join in.

Anjenai lowers her head, and I feel sorry for her having to put up with Phoenix's antics.

"Grow up," I whisper with a look of warning.

"What?" she asks, sliding on her innocent act. "I'm just saying between school, football practice and me, when will you have the time?"

"I'll make time," I stress and then look back at Anjenai. "I mean it. I'll do it. I don't mind."

Anjenai's pretty gaze bounces between me and Phoenix. Finally, she tilts up her chin. "I'd like that."

"Good, then it's settled," I say.

Coach Whittaker gives me a thumbs-up and a relieved smile. "Thanks, Romeo."

"No need to thank me." I glance at Anjenai. "I'm actually looking forward to it."

chapter 9

Anjenai—Be Still My Heart

the rest of the school day floated by like a dream. Romeo is going to teach me how to play basketball. Me. Alone with him. I can't believe it.

Suddenly, I'm not so worried about the principal's call to Granny, my Saturday detention and the BFF's fight with the Red Bones. Unfortunately, my girl Tyler doesn't seem so excited for me anymore.

Of course I know why. It's strange. She's busy pretending not to care while I'm busy pretending not to notice. What else can we do? For the first time in our lives, the three of us like the same boy when in reality we have about a snowball's chance in hell of luring him away from the most popular girl in the whole school.

Climbing back onto Mrs. Barksdale's bus, I quickly crash back down to reality. Billie Grant might have spent her first day of school at the hospital with a broken nose, but her crew was sitting huddled at the back of the bus waiting, it seems, for the BFFs to make their appearance. The moment they spot me, their eyes blaze a hole straight through me.

How did I forget about them?

And why, oh why, didn't I wait for my girls before I raced out here? My first impulse is to sit at the front and not go anywhere near the back. It's not that I'm scared; it's just that I'm in enough trouble. Seeing how everyone is watching, I boldly walk toward the center of the bus with my head up, ready to throw down if the situation is necessary.

I toss my backpack into an empty seat and finally sit down.

"Yeah, you better not come back here," one of the girls shouts.

I turn around in my seat and toss her the bird.

The other kids on the bus snicker and laugh.

While I wait for Kierra and Tyler, I glance out my window toward the front of the school, where some parents pick up their kids, and see the Red Bones talking and laughing like they don't have a care in the world.

Though I can't stand them, I can't help but wonder what life must be like for them. According to Nicole, Phoenix's family is obscenely rich, and her parents give her free rein to do whatever she wants. I can't even wrap my brain around that.

It's clear most of the girls at Jackson High envy them, despite their constant talking behind people's backs, and I'm beginning to wonder if I'm one of them. The idea of going where I want, buying what I want and being draped on Romeo Blackwell's arm didn't seem like a bad life to me.

Kierra rushes onto the bus and races to my side.

The girls in the back boo and hiss.

Kierra glances up and shoots off two birds. "Losers," she shouts and then returns her attention to me. "You'll never guess what happened to me!"

"No. You'll never guess what happened to me," I say. "But you first."

"You know that boy Romeo?"

I stiffen, my smile suddenly feeling strained. "Yeah."

"Well, remember I told you our lockers are next to each other, right?"

I bob my head.

"After lunch, he comes up to me and apologizes for his lame friend dissing my outfit and *then* he tells me that he thinks my outfit is cute!" She grabs my hand and begins bouncing in her seat. "Can you believe it? He actually said I was cute!"

I blink at her. "Cool. That's great," I lie.

"Okay. Your turn. What's your news?"

For a split second I debate whether to share my news, but then I perk up. "It's about Romeo, too," I tell her.

"Oh?"

"Yeah." I quickly tell her what happened in the gym, right down to the part where Romeo had offered to give me a few basketball lessons.

"You're kidding me." Her eyes seem to freeze up.

"No. It was like the most amazing thing I've ever done. I'm seriously thinking about joining the team this year."

"No, I mean...he seriously offered to give you private lessons?"

I nod.

"You're actually going to be alone with my future boyfriend?"

"What?" I laugh.

"Well, I mean...I like him."

"I hardly see how that matters any. I like him, too," I tell her.

"We can't like the same boy," she tosses back. "It's in the rule book."

"No it's not." I drop her hand. "You just made that up."

"Well then it *should* be a rule."

"A couple years ago we both had crushes on Nick Cannon."

"That's not the same," she snaps.

"Why not?"

"What are the chances of us ever meeting Nick Cannon? I'm talking about a real boy that we both know and want to..." She glances around and leans forward to whisper, "Date."

"You mean the same boy that already has a girl-friend?" I remind her.

"Ex-girlfriend," she says, smiling. "Remember, Nicole said that they broke up."

I glance out the window to where I'd seen Phoenix standing. Now Romeo was there, laughing and talking. "They don't look like they're all that broken up to me."

The bus driver closes the door, and Tyler is shouting

as she runs toward us. The door reopens, and Tyler jumps on with a smile.

"You almost didn't make it," Mrs. Barksdale says, closing the door and pulling away from the curb.

Tyler just rolls her eyes and heads back toward us. Special note, there's no booing and hissing at her. "Hey, what I miss?" she asks, dropping into the seat in front of us.

"Nothing," Kierra and I lie, scooting to opposite sides of our seat and crossing our arms.

Tyler lifts a curious brow. "Sure doesn't look like nothing."

"Well it is," I reinforce. Not liking one bit that I am withholding anything from a member of our group. As far as I can remember we've never kept secrets from one another, but something tells me that if I include Tyler into our discussion, it could stretch into a three-way argument. Assuming I'm right about Tyler's secret crush on Romeo, too.

Tyler holds my gaze for just a second. Something tells me that she knows I'm lying; but instead of calling me on my b.s., her gaze shifts to the back of the bus. "Whatcha lookin' at?"

I glance over my shoulder and see the other girls go back to mindin' their own business.

"Were they bothering you?" Tyler asks.

"No," I lie again. "Just let it go," I tell her. "We can't come to school every day tryin' to beat people up."

She shrugs. "Why not?"

"Because it's not exactly how I envision my high school years."

"C'mon." She smiles. "You always said that you wanted to be popular."

"Popular because people like us, not because they fear us. Pretty soon we're not going to be any better than Billie Grant and those jerks in the back."

"But we only beat up people who deserve it. Billie deserved what she got."

Kierra snickers. "She has a point."

"What about the Red Bones? We could've given them their table."

"It wasn't theirs."

"And the guys?"

"They were rude to Kierra!"

What was the point of arguing with her?

"You know my dad always says if you never stand for anything, you'll fall for everything."

"Yeah. I guess," I agree. "Still Granny is going to kill me when I get home and I tell her I have Saturday detention."

"You mean if she doesn't already know."

I groan.

Thirty minutes later, our bus arrives at Oak Hill apartments, and as we march home we share the details of our first day at school. Come to find out, Coach Whittaker had also approached Tyler about trying out for the team.

"Are you?" I ask, jumping with excitement. "It'll be great if we're both on the team."

"Umm...I don't know." She shrugs. "I'll think about it." It doesn't escape me that *she* had asked me earlier *before* Romeo promised to give me private lessons.

"Maybe you should try out, too, Kierra," I say, switching tactics.

"Me? Basketball? You done fell and bumped yo head." She laughs. "Running up and down the court and sweatin' out my perm. Chile, please." We walk a ways before she adds, "You know I did see a flyer for two spots on the freshman cheerleading squad. Maybe Tyler and I can try out for that instead? We can be on the side court cheering you on."

Tyler is laughing before she finishes her sentence. "Me in a short skirt with pom-poms? Now who has fallen and bumped their head?"

Kierra and I think about it for a moment and then burst out laughing.

"Okay. It's not that funny," Tyler says sourly.

"Oh, yes it is."

"All right," Kierra amends. "You two join the basketball team, and I'll be on the sidelines. BFFs still together."

I glance at Tyler. "I like the idea."

"Yeah, maybe." Tyler seems determined to remain noncommittal.

It's on the tip of my tongue to ask Tyler what she thinks about Romeo Blackwell, but I'm afraid of her answer. I also notice that Kierra doesn't bring it up either, and something tells me she is also debating whether to ask.

"I guess I'll see you tomorrow," I say, since we arrive at my building first. We all wave, and I watch them march off to the next building over.

I enter the building and walk up to the apartment door.

I lay my hands on the knob, take a deep breath and open it. Immediately, my four brothers stop running around the sofa to stare up at me. Robert and Gregory, ten-year-old twins, are the first to yell, "Oooh. You're in trouble."

"Anjenai Legend," Granny's voice cracks out from the hallway a second before I see her hobbling from her bedroom on her cane. "You have a lot of explaining to do."

So much for hoping that the principal had forgotten to call.

chapter 10

Kierra—My Private Hell

The minute I walk through the door, I see my nine-year-old sister, McKenya, huddled on the couch and OD'ing on SpongeBob SquarePants.

"Whatsup?" I ask, closing the door behind me.

She doesn't even look up. "Nothing."

It's a quarter to four in the afternoon, but I know my sister Deborah is fast asleep. She works third shift at the Champagne Lounge so she sleeps during the day.

"Did you do your chores?"

When McKenya doesn't respond, I have my answer. "Turn off the TV, and go do your chores," I tell her.

"After SpongeBob," she says.

"Fine." I roll my eyes. What can it hurt? I slap my backpack on the dining room table and head toward the kitchen for an afternoon snack. However, the moment I enter the kitchen, I see the sink piled high with dishes, and the garbage is overflowing. "I swear. I'm the only one who does anything around here."

Next thing I know I'm taking out the garbage and scrubbing dishes. Forty-five minutes later, I finish and march back into the living room.

McKenya hasn't moved an inch.

"Have you done your chores yet?"

"I'm watching SpongeBob."

"No more SpongeBob." I stomp over and turn off the TV. "Time to clean your room. You've been promising to do it for a week."

"You're not my mom! You can't tell me what to do!"

I shouldn't be surprised by McKenya's outburst because she pulls the same stunt every time she doesn't want to do something. Still, tears sting the back of my eyes.

"Mom is not here. You have to do what I say."

"Nah-uh!" She jumps up with her hands on her hips. "You're not the boss of me."

"McKenya, go clean your room. I *mean* it."

She doesn't move.

"Do you want me to wake Deborah? You know you'll get a spanking," I threaten.

Fake or real tears leap from McKenya's eyes as she finally shoots off toward her bedroom. "I HATE you!" She slams the door.

"Y'all be quiet!" Deborah screams from her bedroom.

I want to collapse in tears or at least try to put on the bubbly face I usually reserve for the public, but I'm too tired. Life is really kickin' me down.

I stomp back to the kitchen, grab the ground beef and a box of Hamburger Helper and start cooking dinner. It'll be late before I can get to my homework. When the food is almost ready, I hear someone shuffling up behind me.

I turn and Deborah is standing in the kitchen doorway. Her hair is standing all over her head, and her pretty face is smudged with yesterday's makeup.

"You're just now gettin' up?" I ask.

She nods and scratches her leg. "Make me a quick plate."

"Sure. Why not," I mumble when she turns and walks off. I swear I feel like Cinderella up here sometimes.

I quickly set the table and fix everyone's plates. "McKenya, come eat!"

"I'm not hungry," she yells back.

I drop my hand on my hip and count to ten.

Deborah is busy shoving food into her mouth.

"Will you please tell her to come eat?" I ask.

Deborah shouts with a mouthful of food. "McKenya, come out here and eat, girl!"

My sister's great parenting skills at work.

"Girl, I'm not playing with you."

Finally, McKenya's door cracks open, and she stomps out to the table. Why did she have to make things so hard? Didn't she see that we were all trying the best we can?

"By the way," Deborah says, glancing up at me. "Your school called me today. What's this about you fighting?"

I sigh and plop into my own chair. "Some girls were talking smack at the bus stop, and it just got out of hand," I say.

"And now you have Saturday detention?"

I nod.

"And how do you suppose you're going to get to school on a Saturday? You know I work a double shift on Fridays, and I'm gonna be too tired to get up and drive you to school."

I draw a deep breath and stare down at my plate.

"I swear you two just like to make things hard for me," Deborah snaps, dropping her fork against her plate. "I gotta jump into the shower. I'm going to be late messing around with you two. I would have been better off if I'd just let you go to foster care." She storms away from the table.

Hatred burns within me, and I try desperately to get a grip. When I finally look up, my gaze locks with McKenya's, while tears streak down both our faces.

chapter 11

Tyler—Lonely Girl

AS usual, Dad isn't home, and I'm glad to have the apartment all to myself. I love my dad, but lately he's become too...clingy. Mom's leaving really did a number on him, and honestly, it's like he's overcompensating for the eight months when she first left, and he drowned himself in alcohol, occasionally showered and never ever remembered to go to the grocery store.

Sad really, since I think his drinking played a part in Mom leaving in the first place.

Bottom line: he forgot about me.

Everyone always forgets about me.

When my parents were together all they did was scream and fight. Never once did they stop to think about me during all of that. Mom would throw things and call Dad everything but a child of God.

Dad would yell and try to restrain her, but once Mom

got going, there was no calming her down. At least now the apartment was quiet.

The phone rings. I check the ID before answering. It's Dad. Rolling my eyes, I already know how the conversation will go. For a minute I debate on whether to answer. Maybe see if he'll worry about me if I don't pick up. But on the third ring, I answer. "Hello, Dad."

"Hey, pumpkin. You made it home."

Yeah. Someone get me a cookie. "Yeah. I'm home."

"How was your first day?"

I shrug. "It was okay."

"You don't sound like you enjoyed it."

"It's school. Am I supposed to enjoy it?"

He laughs. "I know I didn't. Look, pumpkin, I'm going to be working a little late tonight. Are you going to be all right?"

"Aren't I always?"

There's a long pause on the line. Apparently my sarcasm didn't squeak by this time.

"Look, Tyler. I'm doing the best I can. We really need this job right now. You know how the housing market is right now. Construction jobs are a little hard to come by lately."

"Yeah, I know." I feel guilty for having made the comment now.

"Uh, I left a twenty in the cookie jar in the kitchen. Use that to order yourself a pizza. I didn't make it to the grocery store before I headed out today."

Surprise. Surprise. A long and awkward silence hangs over the line before my father catches a clue that I don't have anything else to say.

"All right then. I guess I better get going. You sure you're all right?"

"Peachy keen," I lie.

"Don't do that, baby," he scowls softly. "I really am doing the best I can right now."

I fold my arms and drop into a nearby chair. "I know."

"All right," he says. "I'll see you later tonight. I love you."

"Bye," I say, hoping like always that he doesn't notice I don't say "I love you" back. "See you later." I quickly hang up the phone.

I wipe my face, surprised to feel tears. I pick up the phone again, dial the number for the local Fox's Pizza and order my favorite pepperoni and cheese pizza. After I receive the promise of a delivery within thirty minutes, I notice the flashing light on the answer machine.

I walk over and press Play.

"Hello, this call is for Mr. Jamison. This is Principal Thelma Vincent calling from Maynard Jackson High School. I was calling in reference to your daughter, Tyler…"

I smile at the machine as I reach over and hit Delete. "Nobody cares, lady."

chapter 12

Anjenai—Hoping, Wishing, Waiting

I can't believe it, but the rest of the week went by without incident. I'm actually still looking forward to basketball tryouts next Friday. Also I'm still waiting for Romeo to tell me when we'll be able to practice together. In Spanish class I keep trying to catch his eye, hoping he'll bring it up—but he never does.

"Maybe he changed his mind," Tyler suggests as we walk out of class together.

"Yeah. Maybe."

"You're still a shoo-in for the team. No way Coach Whittaker is going to ignore someone who can shoot as good as you."

I flash Tyler a smile. "Thanks. I needed to hear that." And I did. My confidence needs an ego boost.

"Not a problem." She wraps her arms around my neck. "This is what best friends are for."

It's Friday afternoon, and as we ride the bus home, Kierra is the first to voice the question that's on all our minds.

"So how are we going to get to school tomorrow? My sister made it clear that she can't take us."

I shake my head. "Granny's diabetes has been acting up. She's out the question." We look to Tyler.

"Don't look at me. My dad has been working long hours on his new construction job. He doesn't even know I have detention."

My mouth drops open. "What? You're the one who got into the fight in the first place and your father doesn't even know about it? Didn't the school call?"

Tyler hunches her shoulders. "Yep. Principal Vincent even left a nice li'l message on the answering machine that I promptly erased when I went home Monday."

"Why, you bitch," Kierra barks.

"What? I can't help it if I have an absentee father," Tyler says, smiling.

I just shake my head. "Looks like we're going to take MARTA. We can call and get the bus routes. I'm sure one has to go in front of the school—or near it."

Kierra nods. "I think I should have enough on my bus pass from this summer for a round-trip. Tyler?"

"Sounds like the only option we have."

Riding MARTA isn't as easy as it sounds. To get anywhere in this city on time you have to leave *extra* early. Especially the weekends. Buses tend to run every hour as opposed to the week's every half hour. So in order to get to school by 8:00 a.m., it turns out that we need to be at the bus stop by 5:30 a.m.

Be there—not get up.

At four-thirty Saturday morning, I climb out of bed and try my best to creep around as quietly as I can, but my granny still hears me and wakes up.

Granny, the sweetest woman on earth, is like the fourth member of the BFFs. She's like the only mother figure my three-girl gang has to look up to, and she treats my friends as if they're family.

For the most part, I love hearing her tell stories about the old days. My favorites are the ones about her and Grandpa. How she'd had a crush on him for two years before he ever knew she was alive. Then one day, like magic, he noticed her at a friend's house during a party, and he asked her to dance.

According to her they were inseparable up until the day he died from cancer. Granny sold their small house they used to have not far from Oak Hill so she could pay the hospital bills. Later that same year, she moved here thinking she could make it off Grandpa's Social Security checks. Who knew that a year later she would have to take in her five grandchildren when her son and his wife were killed in a car accident?

When my parents were alive, we too, didn't live far from Oak Hill. At night, sometimes I still dream about our old backyard and, more importantly, my own private room. Now, I sleep on a small daybed on one side of a room while my eight-year-old brother, Hosea, and my six-year-old brother, Edafe, sleep on the opposite corner of the room in bunk beds. The twins sleep on a sofa pullout in the living room. My point is we're all packed in Granny's apartment like sardines in a can.

When my parents died, they were driving back to Georgia from a casino in Tunica, Mississippi, after celebrating their fifteenth wedding anniversary. The police said a driver of an eighteen-wheeler truck had fallen asleep behind the wheel. His truck had crossed over into their lane and hit my father's Ford Explorer head-on.

Me and my brothers have been living with Granny ever since.

"Hey, baby," Granny says shuffling into the kitchen behind me. "You have time for breakfast?" She opens the refrigerator and peers inside. "I can whip you up some eggs and bacon."

I glance at the clock on the stove. "That's all right, Granny. I'm just going to grab a cereal bar."

"I don't mind. It won't take but a few minutes."

"No, Granny. I really don't have that much time." I smile at her. Granny is always looking for a reason to cook.

"Did you already pack your lunch?"

"Yes, ma'am." I rush over to her and kiss her on the cheek and then hurry out of the apartment. Once I step out of the building, I see Tyler and Kierra dragging their way toward me.

"I'm so tired," Kierra complains.

"You look it. Didn't you get any sleep last night?"

She just grunts and gives me a look telling me to back off. I smile and look to Tyler; it's clear that she's not exactly up for conversation either.

"Guess what," Kierra says, trying to perk up after we climb onto the MARTA bus.

"What?"

"My sister says I can try out for cheerleading long as it doesn't mess with my grades and I still get my chores done."

"How did you pull off that miracle?" I ask.

"I know. Right?"

"Well, I think you're going to be great."

"You think?" she asks, hanging on to my words. "I don't know how I'm going to squeeze in practice and getting to the games, but I figure if there's a will there's a way. So when you girls make the team, I'll be right there cheering you on."

"Please," Tyler mumbles. "You just want to be a cheerleader so you can cheer and root for Romeo at the football games."

Both Kierra and I are stunned by the bitterness in Tyler's voice.

"That's not true," Kierra sputters.

"What's up with you?" I ask Tyler.

"What?" she asks, brushing her hair back from her face. "I'm just stating the obvious."

"Oh, really? It sounds more like you're being a bitch to me," Kierra challenges.

"All right. Calm down," I say, noticing we were drawing a few unwanted stares our way.

Kierra and Tyler sulk and glare at each other.

"You girls know the rules," I remind them. "No guys get in between *us*."

"Ha!" They bark and shift their glares toward me.

"You're a fine one to talk," Tyler accuses. "Oh, Romeo, can you teach me how to play basketball?"

I shift in my seat, hurt. "I never said that. He offered!"

"Whatever." Tyler rolls her eyes.

"You know what? You're just jealous because he's going to be spending time with me and not you."

"Ha!"

"Don't *ha* me. You know it's true. I know you're only pretending not to like him. You're not fooling anyone."

"Look, if I wanted Romeo, I could get him."

"In your dreams." Kierra laughs, leaping into the conversation.

Okay. Now at this point I can't remember how this argument even got started, but it's one that I suddenly feel I can't lose.

"All right. How about we make a bet," Tyler suggests, sitting up in her seat.

"What sort of bet?" I ask.

"On which one of us can get Romeo."

"That's easy," Kierra says. "None of us. He's with video-vamp-wannabe Phoenix, remember?"

"Does that mean you're chickening out?" Tyler asks.

"I'm not chickening out."

"Good that makes two of us." Tyler turns to me. "Anjenai, are you in?"

"Girls—"

"Are. You. In?" Tyler asks.

"Fine." I seethe. "I'm in."

We ride the rest of the way to school in silence. When we climb off our final bus, we act like we're complete strangers as we march toward the school building. However, this Saturday goes from bad to worse. Minutes after we walk into the school's library where we have to stay for detention, in walk the Red Bones.

chapter 13

Phoenix—Rich Bitch

This is going to be fun.

The minute me and my girls roll into the spot and see the same three project hood rats who have been nothing but pains in the ass for the past week, it's on. "Well, well, well. Look who we got here, ladies."

"Yeah," Raven says, moving to stand beside me. "It looks like it's our lucky day."

I stroll toward the short chick with the big attitude. "Looks like someone needs to fire the janitor. He forgot to take out the garbage."

Me and the girls laugh.

The hood rats climb to their feet like they're really going to do something. Yeah, I've heard the rumors about Billie Grant before she dropped out of school, but frankly I don't believe a word of it. It's time we let these freshmen know exactly who runs things in this school.

Each one of us square off in front of each one of their pathetic crew. I take my time rolling my gaze over this Tyler chick, wondering which garbage dump she dug her hideous clothes out of. After a full two-minute stare down, the bitch in front of me is the first to speak.

"You need to get your halitosis ass out of my face," she growls.

"Trust. You don't want to pop off nothin' with me." I'm all up in her face, letting her know I can get ghetto right along with them. "Seems to me that you need someone to help knock that chip off your shoulder."

Tyler pushes her face so close to mine that she might as well kiss me.

"Why don't you give it a shot, you little Beyonce wannabe?" The bitch actually flips my hair off my shoulder.

"I'd rather look like Beyonce than—"

"Okay, ladies." A man's thunderous voice fills the library. "Take a seat."

Nobody moves.

"Ms. Wilder," Mr. Palmer calls.

I slowly back away, not sure I want to turn my back on this chick.

"Today, Ms. Wilder," he commands. "Unless you want to spend time with me next Saturday as well."

I finally turn and take a seat. Raven and Bianca join me at my table.

"Ms. Jamison." Mr. Palmer folds his arms as if she's trying his patience.

"Tyler," her friend Anjenai hisses. "Let it go."

At long last, she sits down.

"Thank you." Mr. Palmer sighs. "To show my appreciation for you ladies ruining a perfectly good Saturday for me, I figure I'd return the favor." The vice principal beams a bright smile toward us. "Each of you ladies will write me a ten-page report. Phoenix, Raven and Bianca, your report will be on the dangers of smoking."

I roll my eyes. "But we weren't smoking," I lie. "That security guard couldn't prove a thing."

"This isn't a courtroom, Ms. Wilder," he says impatiently. "You'll do the report anyway."

"Jerk," I mumble under my breath.

Mr. Palmer turns to the other group of girls. "Anjenai, Kierra and Tyler, you ladies will do a ten-page report on school violence."

They fold their arms and stare back at Mr. Palmer.

"And so you know, I expect six-different reports." He glances around the room and looks each of us in the eye. "Am I understood?"

No one says anything.

"Am. I. Understood?" he asks again.

We all mumble and groan, but there's not a *yes* to be heard.

"Good." Mr. Palmer nods in approval. "You can get started now." He turns and glances up toward the clock on the wall. "We're going to treat today like a regular school day. You'll work on your papers until noon. We'll take a lunch break and pick back up at one o'clock." He looks back over at us. "I need to run to my office and pick up a few things. I trust you ladies will be on your best behavior while I'm gone." When that didn't get a response, he adds, "No fighting. Any fighting will result in a month of Saturday detentions. Am I clear?"

Silence.

He sighs. "Am. I. Clear?"

We grumble and moan again.

"All right. I'll be right back." He walks backward for a few steps as if he's afraid to turn his back on us.

However, the minute he's out the door, we're all back on our feet and in each other's faces. Tyler is the first to shove me, and I shove her back. Next thing I know I hit the ground and this girl is all over me.

I've never seen anyone move so fast. I barely get in a few licks before I feel Tyler's body being dragged off of me.

"Quit it, you guys!" the other girls scream. "Quit it. Mr. Palmer is going to be back here any minute."

Raven and Bianca help me stand, and I touch my lip to see if I'm bleeding. "You bitch," I seethe. "This isn't over, you project bitch."

"Anytime," Tyler says as her girls pull her back to her seat. "Maybe I'll snatch the rest of that weave outcha head."

My hand automatically flies to my hair to check the tracks.

Her girls laugh.

"Whatever. At least my man loves me just the way I am," I toss back in her face. Just as I suspect, that shuts her up. Yet, at the same time, I can't help but smile at her foolish ass. "You like Romeo, don't you?"

She doesn't say anything.

"Yeah." I nod. "I've seen how you look at him—checkin' him out."

My girls giggle.

"Pathetic. Do you really think you stand a chance against me? A little girl like you? What are you thirteen, fourteen?" I laugh. "Trust me, honey. Romeo needs a real woman. Someone who can give him what he needs. He's not going nowhere."

My girls give me high fives.

"You can look, but you can't touch," Bianca warns.

"Maybe you need to tell him that," Tyler says, crossing her arms.

For a brief moment, my heart flutters.

"If he's yours then why is he always up in my space cheesing?"

"You're lying?"

"Am I? Maybe you need to ask your sister, Nicole, the real deal."

"Nicole." I laugh. "Please, that bitch lies on the regular. You're a fool to believe anything she says."

She only shrugs, but her smile bothers me. "Then you have nothing to worry about."

I wish that was true. But lately Romeo has been acting strange. We had a little fight just before school started. So technically we broke up. But it's no big deal. We break up and get back together all the time.

This time will be no different.

I think.

I hope.

My gaze drifts over Tyler again and then toward her two friends. Hadn't I seen Romeo alone with each of these girls in the past week?

Wait. What am I thinking? Look at them. Why would Romeo have chicken when he could have steak? They aren't a threat to me. Romeo and I have a bond. After dating four years, we know everything about each other: our dreams and secrets. We've been through a lot together. Plus, I had given him my virginity. Romeo is mine.

He will always be mine.

I'll make sure of that.

chapter 14

Romeo—Restless

"I think me and Phoenix are finally over," I blurt out to my boys, Chris and Shadiq, in the middle of our Grand Theft Auto game.

They only laugh and continue playing.

Now that the words are out of my mouth, I feel this huge burden being lifted off my shoulders. "Nah. I mean it," I insist.

"Aw. C'mon, bro. You gotta be kidding me, right?" Chris asks. "Damn," he exclaims as his man is killed on the screen. "Now, look at what you done made me do."

"Your ass was losing before that," Shadiq chuckles, shutting off the game.

"Y'all want some more snacks?" I ask, standing from one of the game chairs and exiting my bedroom. Just like two lap dogs, my boys follow me downstairs to the kitchen.

"Yo, you're really thinking about ending things with Phoenix for real this time?"

"We already broke up. I don't think we'll get back together."

"Come on," Chris says. "We're talking about the hottest chick in school. Why the hell would you want to walk away from that?"

"I'm just not feeling her right now," I admit.

"Do you know how many boys are dying to get your spot right now? Hell, I wish I could date her."

Shadiq punches Chris's shoulder.

"Ow!" Chris turns and rubs his shoulder. "Why the hell did you do that?"

"You don't tell your boy that you want to kick it with his girl. What's wrong with you?"

"Yeah. That's pretty foul," I tell him, grabbing potato chip bags out of the cabinet.

"Sor-ry," Chris says, rolling his eyes. "But I was just being honest and trying to let my man know what a good thing he has going."

"A good thing? I feel like an accessory on Phoenix's arm while she prattles away about clothes and makeup—stuff that just bores me to tears. We're just too different," I confess. "We don't have anything in common anymore."

"You're still hittin' it, ain't you?" Shadiq asks.

I shrug a *so what* at them.

"Hell, then what else do you need to have in common?" Shadiq asks.

"There should be more to a relationship than just sex," I say, and then I meet two blank stares.

"What?"

"Boy, get the hell out of here!" Chris laughs.

"Very funny."

"I'm not trying to be funny. Man, we're fifteen. We're only supposed to have one thing on our minds."

"Two," Shadiq corrects. "Sex and sports."

"Yeah, and if we're lucky to make the NFL then it will open the doors for even more sex."

"I'm talking to a bunch of idiots," I say.

"No. You're talking to two realists. Nobody expects us to be all deep and shit at this age. Save that bullshit for when we get all old in our thirties and are looking to get married. Right now, we're supposed to be young and dumb and I, for one, intend to be just that."

"Where in the hell do you get this stuff from?" I ask.

"My dad," Chris says. "After high school he says girls get *real* complicated."

They're complicated now, but I don't tell them that. I'll let them discover that on their own.

"Look," Shadiq jumps in. "You and Phoenix are the 'it' couple in school right now. Nobody even comes close. You're going to dump her for who? Bianca…Raven? They are the only other fly chicks up in there."

"Hey, I'm feeling Raven right now. I love the way she says *papi* all the time," Chris says.

"And if everything goes according to plan, I'm going to be hittin' my own home run with Bianca tonight," Shadiq boasts.

"No shit? You two are going out?" I ask, surprised. Bianca only showed love to the white boys.

"Yep. And a brotha like me plans on gettin' in where he fits in. Believe that." Shadiq holds up his hand for a round of high fives.

"See, this is how it's supposed to be—the three of us with the Red Bones. The hottest playas with the finest chicks. We can't be stopped, son."

I shake my head and turn to the fridge. I reach for the sodas, but my boys are there in a heartbeat and grabbing my dad's beer. "Whatcha doin'?"

"Relax," Chris says. "Your dad isn't going to miss a couple of bottles."

"Yeah, he has two cases in here." Shadiq pops open his can and takes a long swig. "Aah. Now that hits the spot." He reaches back into the fridge and tosses me one. "Bottoms up."

I hesitate. We started sneaking and drinking beer this past summer. It was first out of curiosity, and now I think it's because Chris and Shadiq think it makes them feel grown. Me? I didn't care for the taste at first, and now I've gotten past it. The problem is: once I get started I can't seem to stop. Sometimes I get mean.

Sometimes I black out.

The guys always say I'm hilarious when I drink. I just know I feel awful the next day.

"What? You're not going to drink with us?" Chris asks.

"C'mon," Shadiq says, then downs another gulp. "You need to loosen up. Talkin' about dumpin' Phoenix and shit. You know what your problem is?"

"I have a problem now?"

"Damn right. You *think* too much."

"Amen to that." Chris smiles. "You're a lot more fun when you drink."

"Funny. You stay the same asshole."

They laugh, and we grab our snacks and beer and return to my bedroom. When Shadiq starts up the game again, Chris returns to our previous conversation. "So if you're seriously thinking about dumpin' Phoenix, who're you thinking about replacing her with?"

I shrug. "I dunno. Maybe I'll be a free agent for a while."

They laugh again.

"C'mon, Romeo. We're your boys. You don't drop someone like Phoenix from the roster without having a replacement in mind. That's dick suicide."

Instantly, tough talkin' Tyler Jamison pops into my head and then the sweet face of Anjenai from gym class. "Nah. I don't have anyone in mind," I lie.

"Then let's find you someone," Shadiq says.

"What? Put up a want ad or something?"

"We can post it on Facebook or MySpace," Chris suggests.

"Or not," I say. "I'm not hard up, fellas."

"Maybe not, but with homecoming seven weeks away, everyone is looking to couple up right now," Shadiq says after dying again on the screen. "Matter of fact, maybe you should wait on breaking things off for good until after homecoming. Phoenix is probably going to be Homecoming Queen, and you, being the most popular guy in school, are going to be King. You're just going to wind up being with her anyway."

Believe it or not, that actually makes sense to me. "I don't know." I was hoping to uncomplicate my life before then. "I'll think about it," I say and finally take a sip of beer.

chapter 15

Tyler—Too Cool For School

BY the time Mr. Palmer returns to the library, we have scrambled back to our seats; but our gazes continue to shoot daggers. I'm beginning to think that it might be worth a month of Saturday detentions to just finish what we started. Someone needs to teach these high yellow bitches a thing or two with their fake highlights and the layers of MAC makeup.

This first week of school has been hell in part because of the Red Bones gossiping and spreading lies around the school. I ain't going out like that. If these girls want to throw down then I'm down with it. Believe that shit.

I'm sick of these bitches.

Saturday detention creeps by like a turtle running the Peachtree Road Race. It's mind-numbingly dull. It takes all of twenty minutes to write Mr. Palmer's b.s. of a report. The rest of the time, I remain ready to rumble at the slightest indication.

Dad has been talking to me lately about seeing someone about my anger issues. Frankly, it wouldn't be an issue if everyone just stopped trying to piss me off all the time. Besides, he's a fine one to talk about someone gettin' help.

There's no talking allowed in Mr. Palmer's Saturday detention, so the Red Bones just text each other and giggle while the BFFs pass notes the old-fashioned way. This is just another example of how the Red Bones and the BFFs are as different as night and day.

They are high class. We're low class.

They are rich. We're poor.

They fight by spreading gossip and lies. We knuckle up and throw down.

When detention is finally over, Mr. Palmer insists on walking everyone out of the building. I think he just wants to make sure the two groups don't kill each other on his watch.

Smart man.

The BFFs humiliation is complete when a fancy Range Rover arrives at the school to pick up Phoenix and her friends while we stand across the street at the city bus stop.

"The haves and the have-nots," Kierra says as we watch them drive away while pointing and laughing at us.

"I can't stand those bitches," I mumble.

"You know what else they have?" Anje says, folding her arms. "Romeo. At least Phoenix does anyway."

I think back on that crazy bet we made this morning and laugh. "We were being stupid, huh?"

"Retarded, more like it," Kierra chimes in. "Were we really fighting over a boy this morning?"

"Worse," I say. "A boy with a girlfriend—a bitchy girlfriend."

"I don't know what he sees in that girl," Anje says. "My brothers have more breasts than she does."

"I do," Kierra says. "Do you see the clothes that girl rocks on the regular? Those jeans alone are worth more than my sister's car payment."

Anjenai and I roll our eyes.

"Other than when you were trying to snatch the hair off her head this morning, the girl has been flawless all week. What guy wouldn't want that on his arm?"

Kierra's words are like a sock in the gut. My clothes in comparison deserve a violation ticket from the fashion police.

"Whatever." I shrug. "I have better things to do with my time than spend hours on hair and makeup before I step out of the door every morning. No offense, Kierra."

"It doesn't take hours—especially if you get the good stuff. Maybe you should come over tomorrow, and I can give you a makeover."

I glare at her.

"Or not."

"No, thanks. My beauty regimen is Sea Breeze and ChapStick. A winning combination, if you ask me."

"So what are we saying?" Anje asks. "Are we squashing that stupid bet?"

"Absolutely," Kierra says. "No guy is worth us fighting over."

This is true. "You're right. I was just grumpy this morning."

"You're grumpy every morning." Anje laughs.

"True," I admit, laughing along with her. Though I'm happy me and my girls are making up, I still have this one problem. I genuinely like Romeo. A lot.

I just don't know how to show it.

It doesn't matter. I'd ruined any chance with him by treating him like he was something stuck on the bottom of my shoe. In my defense, that's how I've always treated boys. If I like them, I punch them. It's weird, I know. It used to work back in elementary school. The rules changed when I wasn't looking.

"Maybe we should make a new BFF rule," I suggest.

"What new rule?"

"Well, how about if there's a boy that all three of us likes then none of us can date him?"

They hesitate.

"Think about what just happened with us this morning. We were about to break up a fourteen-year friendship because we wanted one boy for ourselves. What if it happens again?"

"She has a point," Kierra says, turning to Anje. "Besides, there are plenty of cute boys to go around."

Anje nods. "All right, it's officially a new BFF rule, which means none of us will ever date Romeo Blackwell."

I hold out my hand and watch theirs fall on top of mine as we shout, "Deal!"

chapter 16

Leon Jamison—Single Father Blues

NO matter how hard I try, I just can't seem to crawl out of bed. I've been working for forty-one straight days, trying to pocket as much dough as I can in these hard economic times, but I just can't do it this morning. Every inch of my body aches, and my mind is more than a little hazy from the six-pack I polished off last night before passing out on this cheap-ass couch. I groan and manage to sit up. Even though I'm fairly certain I'm in my own house, it takes me a moment to recognize the place.

For a few long minutes, I just sit there scratching the side of my ass and try to think. Since I'm obviously taking the day off, I try to think about what I want to do. I glance around the living room and frown at the trash piled around the place. Jesus, doesn't Tyler ever clean up around here?

Tyler. Humph. Maybe I should do something with her today. Lord knows I can't remember the last time we actually spent time together. Hell, who am I kidding? Tyler is a teenager now, and it's not exactly cool to spend the day with your old man.

Old man. Time is cruel.

Somehow I propel onto my feet, though I do teeter a bit, and then shuffle my way from the small, cramped living room and down the hall to knock on Tyler's bedroom door.

I start to twist the knob but then remember the big blow up a few weeks ago about me not respecting her privacy. Despite my paying the bills, Tyler is growing up and filling out—a father's worst nightmare. I guess she has a point about me just walking into her room unannounced. So I knock and wait.

After a minute, I try again.

No answer.

"Tyler, sweetie, are you up?"

No answer.

I draw a deep breath and decide to brave the possibility of a pillow being hurled in my direction for breaking the privacy rule. Instead I'm surprised to see Tyler's bed empty. I frown and glance at my watch. Is it later than I thought?

Turns out, it is.

Great. I'm not about to win father of the year any time soon.

I stumble to my own room and kick my way through piles of dirty clothes to finally make my way to the bathroom and consequently to the shower. I turn on the hot water to full blast. The almost scorching sensation is the only way I can truly wake up—or rather sober up, nowadays. Plus, there's something about the pain I enjoy.

Maybe it's a form of self-punishment. Lord knows I deserve it for screwing up my marriage, my kid, my life. Despite knowing all this, I keep doing it.

Some father I am, huh?

I've been trying to convince myself that Tyler's anger is just temporary—something that, in time, she'll just get over. But I'm not too sure anymore. Her behavior has gone from bad to worse.

I sigh and scrub my skin raw. When I finally climb out the shower, I'm relatively refreshed but still feeling knee-deep in shame for falling off the wagon last night. One hundred eighty days sober shot to hell. No doubt Tyler saw all the beer bottles and me passed out this morning.

I gotta make it up to her.

I toss on some clean clothes and then head out to see if I can find Tyler. Maybe we can just grab some lunch somewhere. Even though a rejection is a high possibility, I still want to spend some time with my baby girl. Despite the fact that she looks so much like her mother, so much like the face of the woman who broke my heart.

I walk out of the brownstone building to see children playing in the streets, darting between cars while teenagers hang out at the half basketball court. I walk around, but I don't see Tyler anywhere. After covering the whole complex and even the local convenience store, I head back toward the apartment to make sure I haven't missed a note lying around somewhere. That's our rule. One Tyler frequently forgets.

As I near our building, a black Celica whips into the lot, and I'm barely able to get out of the way before being road kill. I land flat on my ass and hear a few snickers from a few kids hanging out nearby.

"Oh, I'm sooo sorry." A car door slams, and I hear a pair of heels clack against the parking lot's pavement.

I look up and instantly recognize my neighbor, Deborah, sprinting toward me. Being a man, the first thing I notice is her long, curvy legs, her small, tight waist and, good Lord, her wonderful, trance-inducing large breasts.

"Are you all right?" she asks, hovering above me.

My gaze finally makes its way up to Deborah's small, heart-shaped face and her soulful coffee-colored eyes. My smile is instant. "Yeah. I think I'll survive." I finally peel myself off the concrete and even laugh at the situation.

"Oh, shit. You're bleeding." She grabs my arm.

I frown and glance down at my scraped up arm. "Oh, don't worry about it. I'll live."

"C'mon. We better clean that up," she says, ignoring my protest.

Before I know it, she turns and pulls me along.

"What were you doing just walking in the middle of the street?" she chastises me. "Do you think you have a bumper on your ass or something?"

"I was just—"

"Oh, never mind. Come on." She continues to pull me along. She sure is bossy.

I'm puzzled how she started off by apologizing to me making me feel like I owe her the apology.

"McKenya, did you get that bag out the backseat?" She hollers out toward her nine-year-old sister who's climbing out the car. It reminded me that Tyler could be with Deborah's other sister, Kierra.

"Hey, Deb. Have you seen Tyler today?" Deborah suddenly nearly trips, and I catch her before she takes a hard tumble.

Instead of being thanked, she spats, "Goddamn these shoes."

Again I glance down to her high black shoes, and I have to admit it's a miracle the woman can walk in things that look more like stilts. Either way, she's like a flurry of activity as she manages to grab her purse and bag from the car and usher me and her little sister toward the apartment building all the while mumbling about there not being enough time in the day to get everything done.

Once we enter into their apartment, I'm struck by the differences in our places. Their apartment is immaculate and smells like cinnamon and apples.

"McKenya, go into the bathroom and get me the alcohol and Band-Aids," Deborah instructs.

Little McKenya doesn't appear too happy but drops her plastic bag onto the table and marches off down the hall.

"With a little less attitude," Deborah snaps.

The tension between the sisters suddenly is tense, and I feel like I'm in the way.

Deborah shakes her head and rolls her eyes. "I swear these girls are going to be the death of me." She exhales and seems to remember me standing next to her. "I'm sure you know what I mean. I hear Tyler is a handful, too."

The dig irritates me, and I finally manage to remove my arms from her firm grasp.

"Tyler and I get along just fine."

Her laugh is instant, and her disbelieving eyes lock on to mine. "Is that why you don't know where she is?"

Just who in the hell does this chick think she is? My silence is telling and she laughs again.

"You're no better at this single parenting than I am," she says.

McKenya stomps back into the living room, clinging to a doll. She plops down on the sofa and grabs the remote control.

"Where's the alcohol and Band-Aids I asked you to get?" Deborah asks.

McKenya looks up like she has no idea what her sister is talking about.

"Damn it," Deborah grumbles. "I'll get it myself."

"You know it's not necessary," I say, feeling like I'm seriously in the middle of World War III. "I'm sure I have something to take care of this at home."

"Stay right there," Deborah orders me and for some damn reason, I do exactly as I'm told.

Awkwardly, I glance over at the couch only to have McKenya roll her eyes and then turn up the volume on the television. *Nice kid.*

"Turn that down," Deborah shouts, returning to the living room.

I blink in surprise because in the few minutes that she has been gone, she's changed into a pair of jeans and a plain T-shirt. Now I can see her bare feet with toes painted a vibrant red. I like this version of her better. She appears softer and approachable.

Something flutters in my gut. A feeling I hadn't experienced since my wife walked out on me. I shift uncomfortably on my feet.

"Okay. Give me your arm." She snatches it before I can comply, and I can't help but laugh. "Be gentle with me now. I'm fragile."

A smile refuses to crack her lips as she dabs a cotton ball soaked with alcohol onto my arm. I should've been expecting it, but the sudden burn takes me by surprise and I jump and suck in a startled breath.

"Wow. You *are* a big baby," she says, shaking her head. "Should I kiss the boo-boo as well?"

"No, thank you. Something tells me that your kisses will sting about as much as that alcohol does."

Finally. A smile.

The transformation is stunning.

"You should smile more," I say.

"I will when I have more to smile about." She removes two Band-Aids from the small tin can. "I work nights fifty hours a week where men paw at me and promise me the world while stuffing money in what little clothes I have on. Only for that money not being enough to stretch in this economy."

There's a beat of silence while she slaps on the Band-Aids. Everyone at Oak Hill knows Deborah is a stripper, and for a moment I feel ashamed of how I ogled her legs out in the parking lot. But I'm suddenly aware that I want her to like me.

"Well, I could never promise a woman the world. The most I can afford is a pizza."

Her gaze shoots up. I feel my breath stall in my chest while I wait for the inevitable rejection, but to my surprise those coffee-colored eyes warm. She opens her mouth to respond, but the front door explodes behind me and Kierra and Tyler rush inside.

"I swear I can't stand those bitches!"

I turn and see those foul words are rushing out of my daughter's mouth.

Tyler jumps. "Dad?" She glances from Deborah to me. "What are you doing here?"

McKenya finally finds her voice. "Deb almost ran him down outside, and now he's trying to ask her out on a date."

My face turns red.

"Shut up, McKenya," Deb snaps.

Before I can say anything, Tyler rolls her eyes, pivots and marches out the door.

Just great. I can't win for losing.

BFF Rule #3
Never keep secrets.

chapter 17

Kierra—Rah, Rah, Rah

I **don't** know a thing about cheerleading. It just seemed like a good idea at the time until I walked into the gym and peeped out the competition. Girls are bending and stretching in positions that should qualify them for the Olympics rather than a spot on the freshman cheerleading team.

Back out in the hallway, Anje whispers. "Don't worry. You can do this." She also flashes me a much welcomed smile. The beef over Romeo had been squashed after having to spend Saturday with the much hated Red Bones.

A nightmare.

Of course the BFFs have lost so many cool points for having crossed Phoenix and them. Every time I turn around it seems like one of the many mindless Red Bone followers are going out of their way to either poke fun or spread lies about us. We have no choice but to stick together.

"Kierra! Anjenai! Tyler!"

I look up in time to see Nicole, still our number one fan, racing toward us.

"Are you two here to try out, too?" she asks, coming to a stop next to us.

"I am," I tell her. "Anje and Tyler are just here for support."

"I'll be a part of your support system, too, if you'll be mine," she says.

"*You* are trying out?" At her hurt expression, I realize how that sounded and try to backpedal. "I didn't mean because you're big or anything." Okay, that was much worse. "I just meant...*oh wow. You, too.*" That was a lousy cover, and I'll be surprised if she buys it.

"I think it's great," Anje says. "Of course we'll be your support system. Isn't that right, Tyler?"

"Sure. Why not?" Tyler says though she looks like she would rather be anywhere but here right now. "Rah. Rah. Rah."

"But this means you have to come to our basketball tryouts," Anjenai tells Nicole.

"Absolutely. Well, I tried out for cheerleading last spring. The instructor said I did really well but thought I should lose at least fifteen pounds. I lost ten. Maybe she won't notice."

"Oh. Good for you," I say.

A few minutes later, the next group of twenty girls is called in (meaning me and Nicole). I take a deep breath and then march in a single-file line into the gym. My nervousness borders on having a mild heart attack when I see the cheerleading coach along with three varsity cheer-leaders lined up at the table. Off to the side, another group of cheerleaders are practicing some moves and on the bleachers are more idle cheerleaders. Down in front is none other than the Red Bones.

"Just great," I mumble under my breath. I look back at the gym's door and try to transmit to my girls that I've changed my mind, but instead I get a thumbs-up from both Anje and Tyler.

When I look back toward the bleachers, I see Phoenix and her girls busy buzzing in each others' ears and then start buzzing to the other girls. Tears sting the back of my eyes, and the coach takes her spot in front of the group.

"Okay, ladies, I'm Coach Kennedy, and I'm the head coach for the freshman, junior varsity and varsity cheer-leading squads. Let me take a few minutes to just go over a few points about the eligibility requirements to become a Jackson Eagle cheerleader. We expect our girls not only to be good students but academic leaders…"

Oh, Lord. I hope that doesn't mean I have to have straight A's to be on the squad.

"You must have and maintain a 2.5 cumulative grade-point average to be on the team."

I breathe a sigh of relief. "If you fail a course you will be placed on a six-week suspension from cheering. Two failing grades will result in removal from the squad." She lowered the piece of paper she was reading from. "Alexis and Felicia?"

A tall, perky chocolate girl and her polar opposite, a short, stocky blonde, jumps up from behind the table.

"Okay. Alexis and Felicia are going to demonstrate the routine you'll be doing. They'll go over it a couple of times, and then you'll get to practice with the junior varsity team." She indicated the girls on the bleachers. "After that you'll run through the routine for me to judge and score you. Any questions?"

I have one: can I run out of here screaming without anyone noticing?

"All right. Let's get started." The coach nods to a girl by an old-fashioned boom box to hit Play. Immediately, Chris Brown booms from the speakers. As the girls get crunk, I watch their every move as though my very life depends on it.

When I'm finally able to calm my heart rate, I see that the moves are actually pretty simple. Nothing like the suggestive dance routines my sister practices from time to time at home. Slowly I can feel my confidence build as I watch the routine a second time.

I can do this, I realize while already working my hips. When the music stops, the junior varsity squad spills down from the bleachers.

Phoenix Wilder heads straight toward me.

"Great," I mumble as my stomach twists into knots once again. I take a deep breath and count to ten, but it doesn't work.

"Well, look who wants to be a cheerleader," she taunts, walking around me. "Had I known you were thinking about trying out, I would have told you not to waste your time," she sneers and flips her honey-blond hair over her shoulder.

"I don't see why you even care," I hiss. "It's not like we're going to be on the same squad."

"But you'll be on *my* turf," she sneers.

The music cues, cutting her little speech short. To show that she's a professional, she launches into the routine, making each move look graceful and natural.

I can do that, I coach myself.

At least, I hope.

My heart starts pounding, and I immediately start off on the wrong foot.

Phoenix laughs. "Just give up, and save us all some time."

I glare at her with a silent warning to back off.

"Start on your right foot," she orders. "You do know your left from your right, don't you?"

I close my eyes and feel my burning tears, but by sheer willpower I keep them from falling and making an ass out of me.

"From the beginning," she says with amusement lingering in her voice.

Drawing a deep breath, this time I start on the right foot and perform the entire routine from memory.

When I finish, Phoenix barks, "Do it again."

Confidence restored, I do it again.

Something sparks in her eyes, and I can tell she wants to lie and say that I was awful, but she can't.

"Very good," Coach Kennedy says coming up behind us. "What's your name, hon?"

"Kierra Combs."

She nods and scans her list. "Have you been a cheerleader before?"

"No, ma'am."

"Any dance training?"

I pause. "Well, my sister is a dancer. I watch her some-times," I answer using the term *dancer* loosely.

"Very good," the coach says and then drifts off.

A smile eases onto my face.

"Okay, ladies. Time is up. Let's go through the routine."

I glance over at Phoenix, loving the fact that she looks like she's ready to chew through a box of nails. I lift my head, still smiling. "Thanks for your help."

The junior varsity cheerleaders quickly return to the bleachers. Phoenix makes sure to bump me hard on the shoulder as she passes; but nothing she does now can intimidate me. I'm sure I'm going to make the squad.

The music starts again, and I just go for it: popping my hips, swinging my arms and making my kicks all in sync. From the corner of my eyes I see a few girls struggling, but I keep my eyes on the prize. No way I'm going to show weakness in front of Phoenix and her crew.

No way in hell.

The only time I get a little nervous during the hour-long audition is when the coach starts talking about tumbling. I have no problem performing a basic cartwheel and handstand, but when the coach starts talking about round-offs and walkovers, I'm glancing toward my girls, thinking the coach is talking pig latin.

Thankfully, these stunts will be taught once the lucky few make the team. Overall, I feel extremely confident in my performance.

"Thank you, ladies. Thank you for coming. The results will be posted on the bulletin board tomorrow after school."

I nearly collapse from relief and exhaustion.

"Ohmigod! You were really good," Nicole exclaims as she rushes to my side.

"You were, too," I say, even though I saw her struggling with the moves.

"Naw. I doubt I'll get in. I kept starting on the wrong foot and twisting when I should have kicked and kicked when I should have twisted." Nicole laughs. "I just wished my sister hadn't been here to make me so nervous."

"I wish she wasn't here, too," I mumble.

"What?"

"Nothing."

"Now you, on the other hand, are a natural."

"Thanks." I see my girls moving through the throng to get to me.

"I nearly lost it when Romeo came in," Nicole says.

"What? Romeo was here?"

"You didn't see him?" Nicole asks. "He came in and whispered something to Phoenix. Whatever it was, it couldn't have been good because she stormed out of here. But he did watch for a few minutes. God, he is *sooo* gorgeous."

Damn. I was concentrating so hard on my moves that I missed him. "Wait. You like Romeo?"

"Please." She rolls her eyes. "Every girl in this school has a thing for Romeo. Trust me."

chapter 18

Anjenai—A Change of Heart

I'm ignoring Romeo.

It seems fair since he's pretty much ignoring me, despite his offer to coach me before basketball tryouts. But ignoring him is not easy. Whenever he walks into a room or passes me in the hallway, I'm charged with an energy I can't describe and longing for something I have no business longing for. Every time I think about the argument me and the girls had over him, I want to laugh. There's no way a boy like him would ever kick it with an Oak Hill girl.

What were we thinking?

With basketball tryouts just days away, I'm having second thoughts about the whole thing. What I need to concentrate on is getting good grades. The only way I can fulfill Granny's dream of my going to college is to bust my butt for a high GPA and win a scholarship from somewhere.

Of course I still haven't settled on a career just yet. This week I'm leaning toward being a politician. Someone needs to do something about the way senior citizens are treated on fixed incomes.

"I'll see you at basketball tryouts, right?" Coach Whittaker asks as I head for the girls' locker room.

"Umm, yeah. Sure," I lie. For some reason I just can't bring myself to tell her I've changed my mind.

"All right. I'm counting on seeing you."

In the locker room, Tyler and I endure the buzzing and snickering led by our nemesis, Phoenix. It's strange, really. The day we'd kicked them off their table we thought the whole school was in love with us.

Now not so much.

"See you on the bus," I tell Tyler before parting ways after gym class. I rush to my locker for my English book. I'm so caught up in my own world that I don't notice who's leaning against my locker until I get right up on it. "Romeo."

His beautiful smile slides into place. "I was just beginning to worry that I had the wrong locker."

I glance around to make sure that he's talking to me. When I glance back at him, his smile is even brighter.

"Yeah, I'm talking to you."

I laugh. I feel *that* giddy. "What are you doing here?"

"Well, I *did* agree to give you a few basketball lessons, didn't I?"

"Oh." I blink while my heart starts to pick up speed. "Well, that's all right," I say. "You don't have to do that anymore. I've changed my mind." I step closer and wait for him to move.

His smile vanishes. "What do you mean you've changed your mind?"

I draw a deep breath and try to act nonchalant. "I really don't have the time," I admit. "I really need to concentrate on my grades, plus all my responsibilities at home. I don't know what I was thinking."

He looks genuinely disappointed. "Aw. C'mon. You're a natural. Winning the championship is guaranteed with you on the team."

I smile, and from the corner of my eyes, I see a few stunned gazes swinging our way.

"Ah. There we go. You're smiling. This must mean that you really do want to play."

I want to tell him I'm smiling because of him.

"Well, *I* think you should play," he says. "And I'm not moving from this spot until you agree to join the team." He crosses his arms and smirks at me as if he'd cornered me in a masterful chess move.

"Are you for real?" I ask.

"Straight up."

Even though I'm blown away to be having this conversation, I can't contain my curiosity. "Why do you care?"

"Are you kidding me? Me tutoring Jackson High's newest basketball star?"

I cock my head. "That's pouring it on a bit thick, don't you think? Me? A star?" I laugh.

The first bell rings, and I look up to see students starting to dash toward their classes. I'm going to be late.

"Well?" he probes. "I'm risking being tardy to convince you to do this, you know."

He's serious. He really wants to tutor me.

"I don't know," I hedge, thinking about GPAs and practice schedules.

"Boy. You're a tough nut to crack." He moves closer to me. "What are you so scared of?" As he stares into my eyes I feel as if I'm being pulled into a hypnotic spell, and the last thing I want to do is disappoint him.

"Give me one good reason why you don't want to do this."

He's suddenly standing so close I can't breathe. "Umm. My grades."

"Grades?" He laughs, blowing his peppermint-tinged breath. "You're not going to convince me that a smart girl like you is having trouble with her grades."

"You don't understand," I say, sighing.

"Make me understand."

The second bell rings, and suddenly the hallway is empty except for us. Still, I hesitate.

"Now we're working on an unexcused absence."

"Fine. If I want to go to college then I have to earn a scholarship. To get a good scholarship I need good grades."

"You can also get in with a basketball scholarship."

I hadn't thought about that. I blink up at him.

"You didn't know. Girl, let me school you."

He laughs and then swings his arm around my shoulder. I almost die. Just the feeling of being held up against his chest is like a fantasy come true.

"If you kill this basketball thing like I know you can, colleges will be lining up, begging you to attend their schools. Trust me on this."

"Really?"

"Hey, think of it as a backup plan. If you don't get an academic scholarship then you have a sport scholarship to fall back on. Everybody needs a plan B, right?"

He's making sense. "Yeah, right."

He squeezes my shoulder, and my smile returns.

"So. Are you going to do it?"

I glance up to see he's leaned in close; his light cologne tickles my nose and weakens my knees. "All right," I say. "I'll do it."

"Then we're practicing together?"

"What? Here at school?"

"Sure. Coach Whittaker said we could use the gym."

I'm suddenly suspicious that the coach is the one who put him up to this; but at the same time, I don't care.

"How about today after school?" he asks.

"Uh, today?"

"You got other plans?"

I hesitate. "I, umm—"

"What? Your boyfriend isn't going to like you spending time with me?"

I laugh. "I don't have a boyfriend."

He blinks. "Really?"

"No." Now I'm blushing. "But what I was going to say was that I ride the bus home and if I stay—"

"Oh, well. I can take you home."

"You have a car?" Isn't he like fifteen?

"Yep. I got my learner's permit this summer."

"But doesn't that mean you have to have an adult riding with you?"

He holds a finger to his lips. "A small technicality that my parents have forgotten about."

So I'll be practicing with him *and* riding alone with him in his car. Can this day get any better?

"So. Do we have a date?" he asks.

"Yeah. It's a date."

chapter 19

Anjenai—Private Lessons

I am on cloud nine.

A date. Romeo had actually used those words. Of course I know it's not a real date. The idea of just being alone and spending time with him is enough to plant my head permanently in the clouds.

My next two classes whiz by without me hearing a word the teachers said. By seventh period I can't peel my eyes away from the clock.

"Ms. Legend?"

I jump. "What? Yes?"

Mr. Carson smiles tightly. "Can you tell us who was the third president of United States?"

"Umm, Thomas Jefferson?" I guess.

His smile returns as he nods. "That's correct." He walks on.

I sigh in relief and then command myself to start paying

waiting. Isn't this exciting?" She grabs Kierra's hand and starts bouncing all over the place.

"I know. I'm about to pee in my pants," Kierra admits.

"Oh, please don't do that to us," Tyler quips.

I laugh, but agree.

"I don't know why I'm even bothering to look," Nicole says, diving off her previous excitement so fast it's enough to give me whiplash. "I *know* I didn't make the team."

"C'mon. You gotta be positive," I say in effort to cheer her up—even though I'd be surprised if she made the team, too. Her audition was horrific. She'd looked self-conscious during her routine and had forgotten a lot of steps.

"Well, if you two don't make it," Tyler says, "I guess there's always the pep squad."

"Oh, please." Kierra rolls her eyes. "All they do is wear T-shirts and scream during pep rallies."

"Hey, don't knock it," Nicole says. "That might be my next option."

My heart goes out to Nicole. I've never been around someone who tries so hard to be liked. Other than us, I never see her with other people, and I'm wondering why.

The gym doors open, and the large crowd of girls erupt into cheer. My heart leaps into my throat as I cross my fingers and hope for the best.

Coach Kennedy smiles politely as she maneuvers through the crowd and sticks the list on the board.

"Do you see my name? Does anybody see my name?" Kierra asks.

"Chill. Just wait and see," Tyler says, laughing at her.

attention—but I can't. My gaze keeps creeping [...]
the clock. When at last the final bell of the day rin[g]
would have thought someone had shot off a starter [...]
the way I take off.

"Hurry. Hurry," I tell myself. I don't want to be [...]
I make it halfway to the gym before it occurs to me t[...]
maybe I shouldn't arrive too soon. I might look too eag[...]

"Anjenai!"

I jump and then see Kierra racing toward me an[...]
dragging Tyler behind her. I stare at them wide-eyed lik[e]
I'd been caught stealing out of the cookie jar. How had
I forgotten about our pact to stay away from Romeo?
What will they say if I tell him that I'm now going to be
taking private lessons from him?

"Oh, thank goodness you're here. I thought we'd have
to run all the way to your locker to get you."

"I, umm…" Suddenly, I can't think of a single thing to
say.

"Well, come on." Kierra grabs my arm and starts
dragging both Tyler and I.

"Where are we going?"

"To the bulletin board, silly," Kierra says. "They're
supposed to be posting who made the team, remember?"

"Oh, yeah." I'd forgotten. We race down to the
bulletin board outside the gym where a crowd of girls are
already waiting in anxious anticipation.

"Is my name up there? Does anybody see my name?"
Kierra asks no one in particular.

"They haven't posted the list yet," Nicole's voice floats
over the crowd seconds before she pops up. "We're all

Suddenly, there are loud moans of disappointment in the crowd as some girls even break down and start crying. Is it that serious?

"I'm scared. I'm scared," Kierra chants. "Anje, you go look for me."

I hesitate.

"Please," she adds.

"Oh, all right." I exhale and then begin plowing my way through the crowd.

Teams of crying girls peel away from the bulletin board, and I finally make it through. There are only six spots available, so it doesn't take long to scan the list. I read it. I read it a second time and then turn away.

"Well?" Kierra and Nicole ask when I return.

I hesitate, not liking to be the bearer of bad news. I take a deep breath. "I'm sorry, but only one of you made it."

Kierra and Nicole look at each other.

"I'm sorry, Nicole," I say wincing. The way she looks at me, I feel as if I've just kicked a puppy.

"Well, that means—I made it!" Kierra turns toward Tyler and swings her arms around her neck. Tyler's eyes bulge as if Kierra is choking the hell out of her. When she turns to me, I suffer the same fate.

"I made it! I made it!" she screams. "I can't believe it."

"Congratulations," Nicole says sadly.

Kierra quickly calms down. "Oh, Nic. I'm so sorry."

"Don't be," she says, putting on a smile. "There's always the pep squad." She fakes a smile but then quickly turns and walks away.

"Wait, Nic. You don't have to go."

"No, I—I gotta get going if I'm going to catch my bus," she says and then disappears into the crowd.

The three of us stare after her not knowing what to say or do.

"Damn. I feel so bad for her," Kierra says.

"Yeah. But—" Tyler turns to her. "You *did* make it so that's a cause for celebration."

"I'm down. What should we do?"

"Why don't y'all come over to my place tonight and we can order a pizza and get drunk off root beers?"

"Count me in." Kierra beams before turning toward me.

"Actually," I say, hesitating. "I, umm, have to stay late today."

Their shining faces sour.

"What? You got detention or something?"

"No." I try to think of something quick, but my girls know me and I'm scared they'll see through me when I lie. "I actually need to stay and talk to Ms. Harrison about my biology assignment." That doesn't even sound convincing to my ears at all.

"*You* actually don't understand something?" Tyler asks. "*You* are having trouble with a subject?"

"Someone, stop the presses," Kierra adds, chuckling.

They're actually buying it. "Yeah. I guess I can't be good at everything."

Tyler shrugs. "All right." She turns to Kierra. "I guess that means it's just me and you, kid."

"Damn straight." Kierra perks up again. "But maybe the three of us can do something this weekend?"

"Sure. Absolutely," I say. "We can hang out at the

mall and window-shop. Seriously, Kierra, congrats again." I give her another hug. "I'm so proud of you."

"I did my part. Now you two have to make the basketball team."

I swallow the lump in my throat and try not to look suspicious. "We'll see," I answer, hoping I sound blasé enough. "I'll catch you two later." I turn and run off toward my locker. If I stand there too long, I'm sure the cracks in my facade will show.

I hide upstairs in the girls' bathroom, figuring it is a safe place until our bus leaves the school and I can be sure my girls won't see me creeping back down to the gym to meet Romeo. I'm only in the stall a few seconds when I hear the main door open again.

"Phoenix, calm down."

I freeze at the sound of Raven's accented voice.

"Calm down?" Phoenix yells. "How can I calm down when Romeo has made it perfectly clear he doesn't want to get back together?"

My eyes bug out as I slap a hand across my face.

"He hasn't come right out and said that, has he?" Bianca's high, almost babylike voice asks.

"Pretty much." Phoenix sniffs. "He barely speaks to me at school. He never answers my phone calls or text messages, and in the middle of cheerleading auditions Monday he returned the necklace I gave him last year."

"Whoa," Raven says. "That does sound serious."

"Ya think?" Phoenix snaps.

"Yo, back up, bitch," Raven says defensively. "I warned you of playing too many head games."

Phoenix sniffs. *Is she crying?*

"I know. I know. I know," she whines. "What the hell am I gonna do? I want him back."

"Aww." Her girls say in what sounds to me like fake sympathy.

"I'm sure we can think of something," Raven says.

Phoenix gasps. "What if he's seeing someone else?"

"Who?" Bianca and Raven echo.

"I don't know. But it's gotta be someone, right? That's the only thing that makes sense."

"*Or* he found out about that boy you snuck into your dorm room last year."

"*How* could he have found out about that?" Phoenix asks with skepticism creeping into her voice.

"Not from us," Bianca says.

There's an awkward silence before Bianca adds, "You know, I think you just need to relax. Romeo is probably trying to teach you a lesson for trying to trick him into being jealous with all that booty shaking you did with his boy Chris at my party."

"Yeah. Not exactly the best idea you've had," Raven adds.

"You guys are supposed to be trying to cheer me up not make things worse!"

I hear the door open and high-heeled shoes marching out.

"Phoenix, come back!" Her shadows shout and race after her.

I stand perfectly still trying to digest everything I heard but I can only focus on one thing: Romeo is available and waiting for me in the gym.

Once the coast is clear, I ease out of the girls' bathroom and check down the hallways: empty. I sprint toward the gym with my heart in my throat.

"There you are!" Romeo bounces the basketball once, takes aim and shoots.

The ball glides through the air and then dives beautifully into the basket. "Two points," I say lamely.

He smiles and causes even more knots to tangle in my stomach. God, he looks good.

"I was beginning to think you stood me up."

"Who me?" *Never.*

"Are you going to practice in that?"

I glance down at my standard school uniform of jeans and a cotton shirt. He's wearing a navy-blue sleeveless top and matching athletic shorts.

"I guess I could change into my gym clothes."

He winks. "Good idea."

I start walking backward toward the door. "I'll be right back."

"I'll be waiting."

He makes another practice jump shot just as I back into the door leading toward the lockers. Thankfully, he didn't see the blunder, and I turn and run to get dressed. "God, if this is a dream, *please* don't ever let me wake up."

Rushing and trembling, it's a wonder I'm able to change, but I manage to do the job in less than five minutes. When I return to the gym I'm still stuffing my braids into an elastic band.

"All ready?" he asks, bouncing the ball.

I take a deep breath, still not believing that I'm actually here with him. "As ready as I'll ever be."

Romeo tosses me the ball.

"Let me see you dribble," he says.

Dribble. Okay. I think I know what that means. "That's just bouncing the ball, right?"

He laughs. "Yeah. That's bouncing the ball."

"All right." I start bouncing the ball, patting it with both hands. Turns out dribbling takes a bit of concentration.

"Okay." Romeo walks up to me laughing. "You dribble with one hand. Here, let me show you." He takes the ball and starts bouncing it, passing it from one hand to the next, between his legs and around his back.

"I have to learn how do all of that?"

"Not today. I'm just showing off to impress you." His beautiful lips part into a wide smile.

He passes the ball back to me, and I mimick what I'd seen him do. "Great. You're a quick learner."

"Don't get too excited," I warn. "I still don't think I can do this and run at the same time." I'm not the most coordinated person in the world.

"Don't worry. We'll work at it for as long as you need."

I smile and bounce the ball against my toe and then watch it shoot across the gym. "Oops."

Romeo's laugh rumbles throughout the gym as I give chase. When I return, Romeo decides to give me the simple exercise of dribbling for three counts and then shooting the ball from the foul line continuously.

"We'll attempt running and dribbling on our next session," he promises with a wink.

Is he flirting with me?

I shake the thought off as wishful thinking and continue my dribbling and shooting exercise while Romeo goes over the rules of the game. "You mean people are going to be bumping and shoving up against me?"

"And trying to steal the ball."

"But what if I trip and fall?"

"Try not to." He laughs.

I frown. "This is starting to sound dangerous."

"Trust me. You'll be fine. Here, let me show you how to block." He takes the ball and starts dribbling. "Now you either try to steal the ball or stop me from taking a shot."

"How?"

"Any way you can, but you can't touch me."

Now I'm confused. "How am I supposed to be able to get the ball if I can't touch you?"

"That's the fun part of the game." He smiles and sends my heart fluttering again. "Ready?" he asks.

"I guess."

Romeo dribbles the ball and I launch after it, but he blocks my every attempt. Soon I keep bumping up against his back or his butt at every turn.

That's fun on a whole different level.

He makes his baskets easily. My ability to block his shots feels more like a joke, and my poor feet and hand coordination make me look like a bad string puppet tangled in its own strings. However, I'm having one hell of a workout. Sweat is pouring from everywhere, blinding me on a few occasions.

Then I jigged when I should've jagged and I end up flat on my back, with air racing out of my lungs and pain ricocheting throughout my body.

"Are you all right?" Romeo asks, leaning over my head. "That looked like it hurt."

"No. No. I'm fine. I just suddenly feel like lying here and taking in the magnificent ceiling detail."

He laughs and extends his hand to help me up.

Problem is: I lack the strength to take it. This makes Romeo laugh harder. I love his laugh. It makes me feel like I have a vat of butterflies fluttering in my belly.

"C'mon, lazy bones. You can do it," he coaches.

"Can't we just take a break?"

"Sure. You can get up and go get some water."

"Maybe you should go get it and pour it on me," I say, panting.

Still laughing, Romeo shakes his head. "No dice." He grabs both of my hands and pulls me back onto my feet, but he pulls too hard and I keep going until I crash into his chest and our foreheads bump.

"Oww." I laugh.

"Whoa," he says. "Maybe I should put some brakes on you."

I should laugh at his joke. I want to, but standing this close I'm suddenly having a hard time breathing.

Had someone sucked the air out of the gym?

My heart pumps double time to keep blood flowing to my brain. I notice his smile fade, and there's this invisible energy wrapping around us. Or is it just my imagination?

"So, do you like the game so far?"

I nod because I can't speak.

"I think it's kind of cool when girls dig sports," he says.

I look up and have a hard time resisting the pull of his gaze, and it's all too easy to override my body's warning system, telling me as I lean closer that I'm in danger of making a fool of myself.

Don't kiss him. Don't kiss him.

I close my eyes.

Don't kiss him. Don't kiss him.

I feel his breath on my face.

Don't.

Kiss.

Him.

I stop. "I better go get that water," I say just in the nick of time.

He steps back and nods. "That's probably a good idea."

I turn around and my equilibrium is a joke. I take one step when I feel Romeo's hand on my wrist, and he spins me around.

"Get it later," he says before pulling me back into his arms and kissing me fully on the lips.

I'm in heaven.

chapter 20

Romeo—I Got A New Girl

I'm lost in what has to be the sweetest lips I've ever tasted. I deepen the kiss, slip my tongue inside her warm mouth and then glide it against her own. She moans, and there's something about the way she quakes in my arms that has my body responding.

I don't know what possessed me to kiss her, but I'm damn happy I did. Damn happy.

Pulling Anjenai against me, I can almost hear the snapping of two puzzle pieces. She feels as good as she tastes.

Strange, because up until this afternoon I thought I was feeling her friend Tyler. But there's something about Anjenai that has me caught up. Maybe it's her laugh or just the wholesomeness of her. There's nothing fake about her. What you see is what you get: cute, smart and fun to hang out with.

I like that.

The idea of dealing with a girl without any head games is a major turn-on and just what I need at this point.

Regrettably we have to come up for air. I only pull away slightly so I can still nibble on her full lips. She tastes that damn good. Unfortunately, reality hits her before it hits me.

"Why did you do that?" she asks breathlessly, her eyes still closed.

"I don't know," I admit. "Seemed like a good idea at the time." I pull back and watch as her long eyelashes flutter open. I smile into her clear brown eyes. "I'm not sorry that I did."

"Hey, you guys are supposed to be in here practicing." Coach Whittaker's voice causes me and Anjenai to jump apart and stare guiltily at the coach.

"We were." I clear the frog out of my throat. "We were just wrapping things up."

There's a flicker of disappointment in the coach's eyes, and I know without a doubt she'll be talking to the principal about this. The coach was the one who'd reminded me about my promise to privately coach Anjenai when it appeared she was losing interest in trying out for the team. Now it probably looked like we are just interested in each other.

Which isn't too far off the mark.

"You two better shower and change. I'm locking up in a few."

We obediently nod.

"Sure. No problem," I tell her, rubbing my sweaty hands against my gym shorts.

When Coach Whittaker folds her arms and makes it clear that she's not about to move, Anjenai shoots toward the girls' locker room without glancing back my way.

Is she angry? Had I crossed a line?

Hell, maybe she lied and *did* have a boyfriend. I think on that as I head toward the boys' locker room. Nah. She doesn't strike me as the lying type.

A take a quick shower and change back into my school clothes in record time. The whole while, I'm praying that Anjenai won't just take off to avoid me. I cling to the fact that she said she didn't have a ride home without me, but given the circumstances, she could just ask the coach to take her home.

I hope she doesn't.

Ten minutes later, I run back into the empty gym to wait for her. When another ten minutes passes, I get antsy and fear that she really has given me the slip. For a brief insane moment, I debate whether to peek inside the girls' locker room to make sure she's still here.

Five more minutes pass and I find myself inching my way toward the forbidden door, but then finally it opens and she steps out like a breath of fresh air.

"Hey," I say with relief. "You're still here."

She nods but doesn't meet my gaze. "Still need that ride?"

We stand there in silence for a few minutes. I'm actually nervous.

"You know, I was thinking that I could just ask Coach Whittake—"

"No!"

She jumps.

"I'm sorry. I didn't mean to yell." I clear my throat again. "I'd like to take you home."

"Or I can take the city bus."

I cock one brow up at her. "Is this your way of saying that I'm a lousy kisser?"

"No. No. You were great." She blinks and then clamps a hand over her mouth.

I smile. "Thanks. You were pretty great, too." I've never seen a face grow so red. When she flashes those two adorable dimples at me, I relax. "C'mon. Let me take you home." I decide to push my luck. "We can even stop for something to eat along the way."

She's quiet so long I fear she's searching for a way to politely turn me down. But then she apparently comes to a decision, and our gazes meet again.

"I am a little hungry," she says. "But I have to call home first. I forgot to do it earlier and my granny is probably having a conniption fit about now."

I scoop my cell phone out of my pocket and hand it over. "Here. You can use mine."

She takes it. "Thanks."

As I lead her toward the student parking lot, I walk a few paces ahead to give her privacy for her call. From the sounds of it, she was right. Her grandmother has been worried, but Anjenai smoothes everything over because she ends the call with, "I love you, too. I'll be home soon."

I smile.

"Thanks," she says, catching up with me and handing the phone back.

"Not a problem." We arrive at my car, and I dig through my pockets for my keys.

"*This* is your car?"

I glance at my Shelby GT500KR and then back at her. "Actually, it's one of my dad's. He just lets me drive it to school."

"One of? What are you—rich?" she asks.

I blink.

"Oh, I'm sorry. That was incredibly rude. Please forget I asked."

"No. It's all right." I shrug. "My father likes to remind me *he's* rich. I'm not."

She laughs, and I find myself getting addicted to the sound. I open the door for her and watch her climb inside. Once she's settled, I rush over to the driver's side with my heart racing.

"This is a *nice* car," she says, glancing around the interior.

"Thanks. I'm supposed to get my own car when I turn sixteen," I boast, thinking about a sweet Range Rover, sitting on twenty-twos.

She looks impressed, and I feel ten feet tall. "So. Are you hungry?"

"Starved," she says. As if to confirm this, Anjenai's stomach rumbles so loud it sounds like there's a lion or something in there. Anjenai's face darkens, and her eyes bulge. I can't help but laugh.

"Great. I'm going to take you to my favorite spot— Mellow Mushroom. They have the best pizza."

Twenty minutes later we pull up into the spot, but I feel awkward about escorting her inside. Do I take her hand?

We're in a strange situation. We've kissed, but we're not exactly dating.

I remain on my best behavior as I open her door and then again the restaurant door. The rest of the time, I just have my hands in the pockets of my jeans and try to look as casual as I can. I hope it's working.

I haven't been this giddy in a long time, and there's a certain level of excitement to this whole thing. I've been with one girl my whole life, but now I suddenly feel like a fish out of water. I know from class that Anjenai is smart, and I know from the rumors swirling about Billie Grant that she's as equally tough as her friend Tyler.

Wholesome.

Smart.

Tough.

The combination intrigues me.

"So tell me about yourself," I ask once we settle into a back booth.

Anjenai shrugs and looks uncomfortable. "There's not that much to tell. What do you want to know?"

"Everything. What's your full name? How old are you? Where do you live? How many brothers and sisters do you have? You know, the usual stuff."

She smiles and straightens in her seat. "Anjenai Legend— no middle name. I'm fourteen. I live in Oak Hill apartments, better known as the *hood.*" Her nose wrinkles as she laughs. "I have four younger brothers—all pains-in-the-asses."

I laugh. She sounds funny when she cusses—like it doesn't quite fit.

"Well, I do love 'em, but don't tell them I said that."
Her smile fades a bit for a sec and then she continues.
"My parents were killed in a car accident three years ago.
My brothers and I live with our grandmother now. It's a
tight fit, but we're getting by."

Her sadness literally reaches across the table to me
and I take her hand. "I'm sorry to hear that."

"Don't be. It is what it is."

There's that toughness again. It's so different—refresh-
ing. If Phoenix lost something as minor as her favorite
tube of lipstick I'd have to spend the whole evening con-
soling her. The waiter comes and takes our orders. A half
hour later, our pepperoni and cheese pizza (why mess
with a classic) arrives, and we dig in.

"Now your turn," she says. "What's your story?"

I chase down my first bite of pizza with a gulp of Coke
and then try to remain loose and cool as possible. "Well,
my full name is Romeo Blackwell—also no middle name.
I'm fifteen. No brothers and one older sister. My parents are
alive but incredibly absent, but I see my aunt five days a
week."

"What, she checks in on you or something?"

"Something like that. She's our principal."

Anjenai chokes on her pizza. "Principal Vincent is
your aunt?"

"Yep. You got to love that." He smiles. "She can be
tough but she's cool."

"Wow. Here I thought you were getting all this special
attention because you are the star football player."

I smile. "I had a pretty good season last year as a

freshman. This year we'll have to wait and see. Are you coming to our first game Friday night?"

She shakes her head and eases back into her seat.

"You have to," I say. "I need you to cheer me on."

"You have plenty of people to cheer you on."

"Maybe I want one more."

Her dark gaze meets mine, and I feel this sense of falling off a cliff. "It would mean a lot to me." She sucks in a corner of her bottom lip, an adorable habit I've noticed.

"I don't know," she says.

"There's even an after party at Shadiq's house. Everybody who's anybody is going to be there. You should come."

"I hardly qualify as being one of the cool kids."

"Sure you are. You'll be there with me." I don't know why I'm pushing so hard. I just know I want her there. I want to spend more time with her and explore these feelings I'm having.

"I don't know," she says. "We'll see."

This time, I decide not to pressure her further. I change the subject to tomorrow's Spanish test and then to whether or not Mr. Carson wears a hairpiece. This is a subject of great debate for years from what I've been told.

The hours slip by, and she tells me the story of her and the BFFs. Before I know it, it's ten o'clock and the restaurant is closing.

"Oh, my God. My grandmother is going to kill me," Anjenai says, leaping to her feet. "We gotta go."

We quickly scramble out of our booth and hit the

road. As I'm flying across town, my mind is spinning on how to ask her out again. "So we're going to hit the gym again tomorrow?"

"Maybe," she says fidgeting in her chair. "If I'm not grounded after tonight."

She directs me to Oak Hill apartments—and I have to admit, it's not as bad as I thought it would be. Everyone at school calls Oak Hill "the hood" and I half expected to see drug dealers hanging out on every street corner or junkies milling around. When I don't see that, I breathe a sigh of relief. A thug I'm not. Sure, some of the potholes could be fixed, but for the most part, the place is pretty clean.

"Don't worry. You're not going to get robbed."

I glance over at her in her seat, my face hot with embarrassment. "I wasn't thinking—"

"It's this first building," she says, unsnapping her seat belt and reaching for her backpack.

Great. Now I've made her mad. I pull into a vacant spot and shift the car into Park. "Look, Anje."

"Forget about it."

We're silent for a moment, and then I finally get up enough nerve to tell her, "I had a good time."

"Me, too." She reaches for the door handle again, but stops. "I have a favor to ask you," she says.

"Okay." I watch her expectantly, but she stalls for a few seconds.

"Can we not tell anybody about tonight? I mean, we're just...hanging out. Right?"

I blink at her, stunned. She doesn't want anyone to know that we were together tonight?

"I had a nice time and everything," she assures me.

"But?"

"But, well, I just don't want people to get the wrong impression"

What the hell? I shift in my chair and try to examine what she's not saying.

Anjenai continues. "We have different friends, and I'm not too sure they'll understand what exactly it is we're doing."

"Are you saying that you're embarrassed to be seen with me?" I ask, incredulous. What the hell is happening? Did I just fall into the twilight zone? Here I am thinking I'm feeling this chick and she shoots *me* down? This isn't making any sense. "C'mon. Tell the truth. You have a boyfriend, don't you? You can tell me. I won't get mad or anything."

"No. No. I swear," she says, her bright eyes shining and almost convincing me that she's telling the truth.

"Then why don't you want anyone to know about tonight? I mean—" I shrug and then decide to lay it all on the line "—you gotta know I'm feeling you right now, right?"

Her eyes bulge again, but it isn't until that smile and those dimples hit me that I get my answer. She is feeling me. I turn in my seat so that I'm facing her, and when she remains silent for a moment, I can't help but reach over and brush a few braids off her shoulder.

"To be honest, it's complicated," she admits.

Why do I like that she's playing hard to get? "What would you do if I kissed you again?"

She sucks in a breath. "What? Right now?"

"Right now."

She continues to smile but she looks nervous. "Come here," I say.

Anjenai hesitates a minute, but then finally she leans forward, and when she gets close I tip up the bottom of her chin and finally kiss and savor the taste of her mouth.

This kiss is absolutely amazing, and I can literally feel my heart pounding against my chest. For a fleeting moment I wonder what she would do if I place my hand against her chest. But at the last moment I fight the urge of going too fast. Something tells me that Anjenai isn't one of *those* kind of girls.

When we finally come up for air, I can't help but continue nipping along the line of her bottom lip. She tastes that good.

"We better stop," she says.

"Why?" I ask, fully aware I sound like I'm whining.

"Someone will see us," she whispers.

"So?" I can't help but kiss her again. This time a little deeper. Instead of trying to cop a feel, I pull her up against me so I can feel the rise and fall of her chest against my own. I gotta be honest: her soft breasts give me a hard-on so strong it's about to bust out of my jeans.

Anjenai must've felt it because she immediately jumps back, and I can't help but laugh. "Calm down. It's not going to hurt you."

"I better go inside." She reaches for the door again.

"Wait." I grab her arm. "We still haven't settled this thing about you not wanting people to know about... you know—us."

"Come on," she says. "We travel in different circles."

Now I get it, but just before I open my mouth I think about what my own friends are going to say about me dating an Oak Hill chick and a quiet brainiac one at that.

"All right," I agree reluctantly. "We'll keep this between us...for now." Then I meet her gaze dead-on. "But I meant what I said. I'm definitely feeling you."

Her face lights up, and I find myself smiling again. "Do I at least get a kiss good-night?" Even through the dashboard lights I see her blush as she nods her head. I lean forward and brush my lips against hers. This kiss is just as sweet as the others and equally hard to end.

"Come on. I'll walk you to your door." I reach for my door handle.

"No!"

I jump and then frown at her.

"That's not necessary. People might..."

"All right. All right. You made your point."

"Thanks for understanding." She leans over and kisses me on the cheek. "I gotta go," she whispers with a smile and then jets out of the car and dashes into her apartment building. Maybe she should consider the track team as well.

Still excited, I shift the car into Reverse, but before I pull out, my gaze sweeps across the apartment complex and crashes into Tyler Jamison holding a large garbage bag.

Our eyes stay level for a few long seconds before she turns and walks away.

chapter 21

Tyler—Deceived

I can't believe this shit. That bitch lied to me. I can literally feel the anger roll off of me in waves. Didn't we all make a deal to stay away from Romeo? Now here Anje is creeping and making out in the middle of the night in his car.

His car.

I can't help but stomp my way through the spiraling complex to the public garbage compactor. What the…! What the…!

I reach the large metal compactor, and with one big powerful swing, I send the bag hurtling into the trash. Too bad it wasn't Anje I was tossing in there. Maybe it would make me feel better. I take the opportunity to laugh out loud. Of all the people in my life, I thought I could always count on my girls. Now this shit.

I turn and start to head back to the apartment, but I

stop at the first curb I come to and plop down onto the hard concrete. I need to think. For the first few minutes I can't stop wishing that Anje was standing here right now. I swear to God I would snatch every braid out of her lying head.

Is it too much to ask that you can trust *somebody* in this world? I exhale, shaking my head and then glancing up at the starless night.

Of course you can't trust anyone. Your own damn mother walked out on you.

At the mere thought of my mother, I can feel tears burn at the back of my eyes. But goddamn it, I'm not going to cry over this anymore. But it's hard trying to control my rage. I've been mad at the world for so long that I don't know how to be anything else.

Out of nowhere, a long, steady cool breeze whips through the night. I close my eyes and enjoy the feel of the wind kiss my skin and ripple through my hair. It calms me, but it also makes me feel lonely. I force myself to harden my resolve.

In a snap, the air turns from cool to cold, numbing my nose and ears. I wish it could do the same thing to my emotions. The wish goes unanswered when the wind suddenly dies. Seconds later, I hear a rhythm of shoes slapping concrete.

Someone is coming.

I open my eyes in time to see a couple of girls from Billie Grant's gang approaching. *Just great.*

The two girls spot me, and their laugh cracks the night's stillness.

"Well, well. Look who we got here, Michelle."

"I see it." Michelle looks around. "Where are those two pip-squeaks you hang out with?"

I ignore her.

Michelle laughs again. "I guess it's true what they say, Trisha. The freaks really do come out at night."

"Then what the hell does that say about you?" I ask.

Michelle stops laughing.

"Dumb ass," I mutter under my breath. Instead of scurrying off to whatever rat hole they'd climbed out of, they head my way. I exhale another long breath. "Please. I'm not in the mood."

"Really," Trisha taunts. "Then what exactly are you in the mood for?"

I narrow my gaze. "How's Billie?"

Their eyes mirror my hostile glare. "How the hell you think she's doing? You and your little friends fucked up her nose."

I laugh in their faces. "In that case, tell her there's no need to send us a thank-you note for the vast improvement."

Michelle snickers. "You sure do talk a lot shit for a little girl."

"This little girl is gonna kick your ass if you keep messing with me." I stand. Kicking someone's ass is just the stress reliever I need about now. Michelle and Trisha look me over, and I find myself involved in another staring contest.

At long last, Michelle cracks a smile. "Chill out, Mighty Mouse. Damn. Your ass really think you're all that."

I shoot them the bird and start to storm off.

"Hey, where are you going?" Michelle calls after me.

I don't answer. I don't have time for this kind of bullshit.

"Whoa. Whoa. Whoa. Hold up," Trisha calls after me.

I hear them run up behind me. I don't look back and brace for anything. When they catch up with me, they quickly block my path.

Michelle holds up her hand. "Hold up now. Chill."

I stop. "Get out of my way. I already told you that I wasn't in the mood for this shit."

Trisha smiles. "We just want to ask you if you want to hang out. What? You can't kick it with anyone else but those two loser friends of yours?"

It was on the tip of my tongue to tell them to go to hell when an image of Anjenai and Romeo kissing flashes in my head, and I fall silent.

"C'mon." Michelle cocks her head. "You seem pretty cool. Let's just hang out."

I laugh because that is funny as hell. "Let me get this straight. I kick your leader's ass and now you just want to *hang*. That doesn't make any sense."

"Hey, *no one* is our leader," Trisha corrects me. "Besides, Billie has been foul for a while now."

Michelle bounces her head.

"So I did you a favor?" I say dubiously.

"The way I see it," Michelle adds. "It was going to happen sooner or later."

I keep laughing. These girls certainly don't know the meaning of loyalty. Then again, my own friends have a problem with that as well.

"So what, you girls are going to try and convince to go knock off a convenience store with you or something?"

"You sure are a suspicious bitch." Trisha laughs. "Naw, we're genuinely trying to be nice to you, especially since you're out here looking like a lost puppy and shit."

I look them over again and finally decide *what the hell*. "All right. I'll bite. Where are we supposed to be hanging out?"

"How about over at the playground," Michelle suggests.

"What the hell? Do I look six years old to you?"

The girls laugh. "C'mon. It's not what you think. A bunch of us hang out over there at night."

I frown. It sounds like a pretty damn silly thing to do, but anything is better than going home. "Fine. Whatever." I follow Michelle and Trisha to the opposite end of the complex to the small, pathetic excuse of a playground. There are a couple of swings, monkey bars and a four-foot slide. To my surprise, it's also teeming with kids from school.

"Hey, guys!" Michelle shouts. "Look what we found."

The gang looks up, and I suddenly suspect I messed up.

"What the hell is she doing here?" this boy Kerosene—and no, I don't think that's his real name—asks.

I lift my chin, not about to let them see me sweat. I continue to march in line behind Michelle and Trisha, preparing for anything.

"Chill out," Michelle tells them. "She's cool. She's with us."

All eyes continue to lock on me. Soon a few shoulders

begin to shrug, and then they all resume laughing among themselves.

I move over to one of the swings and eavesdrop on a few conversations. None of them was talking about much.

"Yo, you want a hit?" Someone thrust a cigarette toward me.

I start to shake my head when upon closer inspection I notice that it's not a cigarette, but a joint. My curiosity piques.

"Don't tell me your ass don't smoke," Trisha says, looking over at me.

Everyone's conversation stops, and all eyes return to me.

"I didn't say anything."

"Well, here then." The teenager thrusts the joint at me again.

I hesitate.

Michelle sits down on the swing next to me. "Trust me. Whatever the hell was bothering you a few minutes ago...this is going to clear your mind."

I continue to stare at the joint and then very calmly reached for it.

Trisha smiles. "Inhale and hold," she tells me.

I place the joint in between my lips. A few seconds later, I feel good as hell.

BFF RULE #4
Always keep it real.

chapter 22

Kierra—Peacemaker

"what's up with you?" I plop my lunch bag on the table and sit down.

"What?"

Anjenai blinks up at me like I'd just caught her doing something wrong.

"You sure are smiling a lot lately. You must've aced that biology test you've been staying after school studying for the last couple of days."

"Yeah," Tyler says, easing into the conversation from across the lunch table. "All that extra studying surely must be paying off."

Anjenai clears her throat. "I've told you guys how important it is for me to get good grades in high school."

"Still want to go to Princeton?" I ask.

"I'll take any college," she says. "Beggars can't be choosers."

"As smart as you are, you have nothing to worry about." I bite into my sandwich.

"I'm just a freshman. Anything can happen between now and graduation. I can't take anything for granted."

"I hear you. If I want to make it as a fashion designer, I need to get started now. Did you know Esteban Cortazar got started at our age?"

Anjenai and Tyler just stare at me. I swear they are useless. "He's like the youngest fashion designer ever to show in New York's Fashion Week."

"Oh," they say collectively. But I know they don't care. After seeing the kind of clothes the Red Bones and their minions wear day in and day out at this school, I know it's time to up my game. I don't know exactly how I'm going to afford it, but I can't go out like this. I have a reputation to build. "After watching *Project Runway,* it's clear there's no time to waste in the fashion industry." Seeing their eyes glaze over, I change the subject. "Are you girls ready for basketball tryouts this afternoon? I already have my pom-poms to cheer you on from the sidelines."

"I appreciate your support," Tyler says, "but no pom-poms."

"Hey, guys." Nicole pops up at the lunch table all bubbly and grabs a seat. "Guess what."

"What?" we ask simultaneously.

"I decided to try out for the basketball team, too."

That news is greeted with a wave of silence before I remember my manners. "Oh, that's great," I tell her leaning over to squeeze her hand. It's great to see her bounce back from her disastrous cheerleading tryout.

"Yeah, great," Anjenai and Tyler finally chime in together.

Nicole lights up. "See I figure since I'm not graceful enough for cheerleading that surely I can run and throw a ball, right?"

"Makes sense to me," I say, wanting to be supportive.

"Sure!" Anjenai adds.

"Whatever floats your boat." Tyler shrugs.

The buzz in the cafeteria changes. I look up and see Romeo and his crew finally gracing us all with their presence. I still think the boy is fine as hell. I can't help but sigh and allow my gaze to roam over his tall athletic physique. If I could be so lucky.

My eyes narrow on Tyler. There's something funny about her gaze.

"Too bad we sanctioned him as off-limits," I say, shaking my head and watching the way his face lights up when he laughs. "The things I want to do with him."

"Kierra!" Anjenai snaps.

"What? I'm just being honest."

"Off-limits?" Nicole asks. "What kind of crazy talk is that?"

I quickly bring Nicole up to speed with the pact the BFFs made.

Nicole laughs. "Are you guys for real?"

"Oh, yes," I tell her. "No guy is worth our friendship, right girls?"

"Right." Tyler crosses her arms and then glares at Anjenai.

I glance over at Anje who's busily stuffing chips into her mouth. "Am I missing something?"

"No," Anje answers despite her full mouth, and shakes her head.

I blink at her while the tiny hairs on the back of my neck stand up. Is Anje actually lying about something? Before I can question her, we get an unexpected visitor at the table.

"Hello, ladies."

I look up and nearly swallow my tongue. Here's Romeo smiling and talking...to us.

"Hi, Romeo," Nicole says breathlessly.

"What's up, Nic?"

Behind him Shadiq and Chris are rolling their eyes and looking impatient.

"You girls ready for the basketball tryouts this afternoon?" Romeo asks.

"As ready as I'm ever going to be," Anje answers without looking at him.

I feel those hairs rise again.

"I'm going to try out, too," Nicole informs Romeo. Her eager, puppy-dog eyes give her emotions away.

Chris and Shadiq snicker from behind him.

Nicole's smiling face falls.

"You guys cut it out," I snap. Before I can truly put their heads on the chopping block, Romeo jumps in.

"You clowns behave," he tells them.

Chris and Shadiq sober immediately and stare at their friend as if he'd just grown an extra head. Then Chris catches me shaking my head and asks, "What?"

"You're a real piece of work," I tell him. "Didn't your momma teach you manners?"

Chris's eyebrows shoot skyward as his lips quirk unevenly. "Nah, but if you're teaching, li'l ma, sign me up."

"Boy, I ain't got time to upgrade you."

"Oh, shit," Shadiq barks. "She just told you."

Chris laughs and actually strikes an adoring pose, causing my stomach to flutter beneath his amused gaze. "Yeah, maybe she did." He looks me up and down, and I feel myself fight back a smile.

"Well, good luck at tryouts, girls," Romeo says, breaking my spell. He pops Chris on the collar and then they roll out.

Nicole slumps back in her chair. "Maybe I shouldn't try out."

"What? Sure you should," I tell her. "Don't let those knuckleheads get to you."

"Yeah," Tyler and Anje chime in.

"Forget them," Anje adds. "What do they know? You'll do great."

"You think so?" Nicole asks, perking up. I swear the girl's emotions swing like a pendulum.

"We know so," Anje says with a reassuring smile.

Tyler crosses her arms. "You two looked pretty chummy."

"What? Me and Chris?" I gasp.

"Not you," Tyler says, turning toward Anje. "I meant *you* and Romeo."

She looks as if she's swallowed a frog. "What do you mean?"

"Come off it. He couldn't keep his eyes off of you."

Anje averts her gaze. Something is up. I hadn't imagined it.

"I don't know what you mean," Anje says.

"Don't you?" Tyler asks. "It's pretty weird for him to just come over here and ask about tryouts, especially since he never gave you those lessons he promised, right?"

My gaze ping-pongs between them. "What is going on?"

"Nothing," Anje says.

"Are you sure?" Tyler asks. "Sure didn't look like nothing to me."

"What's with the inquisition?" I jump in, feeling like I need to come to Anje's defense against whatever craziness that's going on in Tyler's mind this week.

"It's not an inquisition," Tyler says, but still looks irritated. "I'm just asking a simple question about a simple observation."

"It sounds more like an accusation," I tell her. "If there was something going on, Anjenai would tell us. She would never hold out on us." I turn to my girl. "Right?" Secretly I'm hoping she comes clean.

"Right." Anje licks her lips and swallows.

I feel a rush of disappointment, but I struggle not to show it. "See?" I say turning back to Tyler. "So chill out."

"Whatever." Tyler jumps up from her chair and storms away from the table.

I shake my head. "That girl really needs to do something about her anger issues."

Anjenai stuffs another chip into her mouth. "Yeah. Definitely."

chapter 23

Tyler—What About Your Friends?

"I can't believe that heffa lied to my face!" I stomp my way around the school grounds trying to calm the hell down until lunch ends. "This is so foul." I try to come down, but I can't. After all the messed up things that have happened in my life, the two people I thought I could always count on and who would always tell me the truth were my two best friends.

Now that, just like everything else, is just one big-ass lie. Staying after school to study for a biology test my ass. I should've busted her dead in her mouth.

But you know what? This ain't even worth it. I don't need them. I don't need anybody.

"Hey, Tyler. Wait up."

I close my eyes and keep marching.

"Yo, girl. I know your ass hears me."

I stop and turn around. "What, Michelle?" I give her

a look that makes it clear that I'm not in the mood for any bullshit, but apparently the girl is blind because she doesn't pick up the hint.

"Where you off to?" she asks.

"Why?"

"'Cuz I wanted to see if you want to tag over to the school's bleachers for a smoke. I know my ass needs to relax before Ms. Hauss's chemistry class. She's a real bitch."

I laugh. "*You* take chemistry?"

"What? I can't help that I'm smarter than some of these dumbasses roaming around here." She smiles, and it occurs to me that she might even be pretty if she ever bothered to wear makeup.

"So what about it? You down?"

I pull a deep breath and then see Anjenai and Kierra exit out of the school building, laughing. In no time at all I feel my anger rising to the surface.

Michelle turns to see what I'm looking at, and then asks, "What? You and your girls beefing?"

"Mind your own business," I tell her.

"Whatever." She tosses up her hands. "You down or what?"

Anjenai and Kierra look up and see me standing with Michelle. Their smiles suddenly fade.

"All right," I say to Michelle. "Let's go."

I hate liars. I always have. Against my will an image of my mother at our apartment door flashes inside my head. The words *I'll be back in a minute,* are still hanging in the air. The thing is I knew that my mom was lying then just by the way she refused to look me in the eyes. Still,

I waited on that sofa for two days, only getting up to go to the bathroom a couple of times. To my dad's credit, he waited by my side. I think we were both in denial.

Then he started drinking again, and I started blaming him for not going after her. I mean, *why didn't he?* Couldn't he see that she was just testing him?

Parents.

They can be really stupid sometimes.

It slowly occurs to me that Michelle is just steadily yapping away about some nonsense and I find myself just ready to light up and forget about all the b.s. that pollutes my life.

When we get to the bleachers, I see it's the same crowd that hangs out at the playground.

"Yo." Trisha glances up. "You two attached at the hip now?"

"Shut up and give me a hit." Michelle laughs.

Someone else asks me if I'd seen the damage I'd done to Billie's nose yet. "I'm sure it's better than the one she use to have." That actually gets me a few laughs. I try not to smile and then accept the lumpy joint that's being passed to me. This time there's no hesitation on my part. After a couple of tokes, I pass the joint to Michelle. By the time the joint passes around the second time, I'm high as a kite and loving it.

This is exactly what I needed.

A few jokes are told and I laugh. But a minute later, I can't remember the punchlines.

"Shit. I better head back," Michelle says. "Lunch is

almost over, and class is all the way on the other side of the damn school"

A few of the kids bob their heads and start to peel off. I, on the other hand, feel like just hanging out here by the bleachers for a while. Maybe I should skip class.

I lean back on the steel steps, close my eyes and enjoy the feel of the afternoon sun on my face.

"Girl, don't go to sleep," Trisha warns. "Nance patrols out here on the regular. She's worse than a drug-sniffing dog on the police force."

I groan and force myself to stand.

Trisha giggles.

"What?"

"Your ass weaving and shit." She shakes her head as she climbs down the stairs. "You're gonna get busted." Trisha shakes her head and marches off.

I stick out my tongue behind her back. I then continue to flirt with the idea of skipping class but finally decide against it. No more Saturday detentions. Those things suck. I head up toward the school, expecting the end lunch bell to ring at any moment when my name is called out again.

I know the voice without having to turn around. A second later, I hear expensive sneakers slapping the ground.

"Yo, Tyler." Romeo rushes around to block my path.

I try to move around him.

"Okay. You're angry."

"Get out of my way." I move to my right, but once again, he blocks.

"Yo, chill. I just want to talk to you for a few minutes."

"I don't want to talk to you," I snap. This asshole is killing my high.

"Why are you so angry all the time?"

"Because people are always making me angry. People are always *hiding* things and *lying* and then *stabbing* me in the back. And you know what? I'm tired of it." I swallow, feeling tears coming. After taking a few deep breaths, I realize that Romeo is frowning and staring at me. I suddenly feel like a moron.

Drawing a deep breath, I force myself to calm down. "Sorry. I shouldn't have snapped at you."

"No problem," he says tentatively. He suddenly looks as if he's frightened to talk now, but he plunges ahead anyway. "I wanted to talk to you about...you know. What you saw the other night."

The memory of him and Anjenai kissing in his car resurfaces in my mind like it has a million times in the last two days. "What about it?"

"Well." He hesitates.

We both notice a few more people milling about the school grounds. Lunch must be almost over. He pulls me off to the side in front of a large bush.

"I, um, really like Anjenai," he begins, his words stabbing my heart. "She's cool."

I roll my eyes. "Yeah, so?"

"Sooo...as you know, we've been sort of hanging out this week, and she seems to really want us to keep a low profile. I was kinda thinking it was because she fears her friends not liking me or something."

I can't help but laugh at that shit. "So what? Are you asking for my permission or something?"

Romeo ducks his head but holds on to this adorable goofy smile. I swear I want to slap it off his face.

You liked me first!

I grind my teeth together and count to ten before I speak again. "Look, do whatever the hell you want. I don't care," I lie and try, once again, to get around him before tears creep down my face.

Escaping Romeo isn't as easy. His hand whips out and grabs my arms before I can take two steps. I swing back around. "Get your hands off of me!"

He drops my wrist and shoots his hands up into the air as if he was surrendering. "Look, I don't know what's going on and maybe I made a mistake by trying to talk to you, but whatever I did to offend you...my bad." He lowers his hands back down. "Let's just forget this conversation ever took place. Anje didn't want me to say anything, and I don't want to make her angry."

"Ha! Now you want me to keep a secret from my best friend?"

"Well, you haven't said anything so far, and I know you saw us."

I think about this for a moment. "All right. I'll keep a secret if you keep one."

He frowns. "What kind of secret?"

Without thinking I launch up onto my toes and kiss him.

chapter 24

Romeo—More Girls More Problems.

what *the hell?*

This is nice.

But what the hell?

I'm trying to collect my thoughts, but the passion in Tyler's kiss is blowing my mind. Just as I'm getting into it, Tyler pulls back. Still stunned, I stare at her.

"You just kissed me," is the only thing I can think to say.

"OH. MY. GOD."

My heart freezes at the sound of Bianca's voice. I turn around for confirmation, and sure enough, it's both Bianca and Raven. Jackson High's two biggest gossips. The shit is really going to hit the fan now.

The two girls march over to me and Tyler. Their faces stern, their eyes blazing.

"*This* is who you dumped our girl for?" Raven snaps, her accent thicker than normal.

"Why don't you two bitches just go mind your own business?" Tyler squares off toward them.

"This is our business," Bianca's high voice climbs even higher. "Romeo, tell us that you didn't play our girl so you could go slumming. They have better hookers downtown."

"Oh, is that where you work at night?" Tyler challenges.

Raven jabs her hands onto her waist. "No. But I saw your mother there last night."

"Yo, yo." I jump in between the girls, hoping to stop something from poppin' off. "Look. It's not what it looked like."

"Really?" Raven laughs. "Because it looked like you were cramming your tongue down her throat."

"Yeah," Bianca says, her neck swirling.

What can I say to that? It was sort of like that.

"Save the lies," Bianca says. "We saw you with our own eyes. You're probably contaminated now."

Tyler drops her backpack and launches—almost in the same movement. Luckily I'm fast enough to catch her in midswing.

Bianca ducks and then has the nerve to look startled. Doesn't she know not to play with fire? "That bitch is crazy!"

A few people walking in between the buildings stop and gawk at us.

"Y'all are making a scene. Chill," I bark.

"Whatever," Raven says. "C'mon, Bianca. This shit isn't over by a long shot. Believe that. When Phoenix finds out it's gonna be on and poppin'. Trust."

"Bring it on, ho," Tyler yells. "Ain't nobody scared of your bourgie-ass! Who cares about Phoenix finding out? I'll tell her myself."

I groan. How in the hell did I get in the middle of this? "Cool it!" I yell at Tyler, feeling my own frustrations. But Tyler is off the chain. She's still trying to jump out my arms to get to Raven and Bianca. Damn, she's strong. The girl definitely has a lot of passion stored.

"Whatever," Raven says unimpressed. "Just remember you brought this shit on yourself." She then turns her gaze to me. "And you. You know this shit is foul." Finally, they storm off.

"Let go of me," Tyler growls.

"Are you going to calm down?"

"Romeo, I ain't playin'. Get your hands off me."

"Promise me you'll calm down first."

She wiggles a few more times before finally giving up. "All right. All right. I promise."

I weigh whether to believe her and then cautiously let her go. She steps back and tugs angrily at her clothes. When she glares up at me, I'm turned on by the fire simmering in her eyes.

What the hell? How can I be feeling something for her when I like Anjenai?

"Are you all right?"

"I'm fine." She bends down and picks up her backpack. "Those girls aren't going to be happy until we finally have it out."

"Haven't you ever heard of turning the other cheek?" I ask.

"Why? So someone can punch me in the other one? No thank you."

"So you gotta be tough all the time?"

"What are you—the last Boy Scout? I said I was fine. Now leave me alone."

I shake my head. I'm through trying to figure this chick out. "Whatever. You do you, boo. I just walked away from a relationship with too much drama. I'm not looking for more. The kiss, it was nice. But, umm, I think I'm still gonna kick it with Anjenai for a while. Peace." I toss deuces at her and roll out.

chapter 25

Kierra—Oh, snap!

I don't believe it. I literally have to rub my eyes twice, and even then I still can't believe I've just witnessed Tyler and Romeo kissing from the window of my algebra class. I had gotten to the classroom early so I could give my excuse to the teacher why I didn't do last night's assignment; I forgot, but I'll say I left it at home. I had just plopped my books down onto my desk when I looked out the window.

And there they were.

Kissing!

In front of the whole school.

I always knew my girl was bold, but damn. What had happened to all that talk about Romeo being off-limits? Didn't we make a pact? Or did me and Anjenai just get played?

I stand there unable to tear my eyes away from the

scene below—even when Bianca and Raven come onto the scene. I wish I could hear what they were all saying. It looks pretty heated. Other people are stopping and pointing. And predictably, Tyler launches toward the girls. Romeo restrains her effortlessly.

I shake my head. What kind of crazy world is this when a feisty, tomboy can get a boy like Romeo Blackwell? It just doesn't seem fair, if you ask me.

At long last the first bell rings. I finally pull my eyes from the window to see Mr. Griffin stroll into the class.

"Ah, Ms. Combs. You're in here early."

I quickly plaster on a fake smile and rush up toward his desk. When I give my excuse for not having my homework, Mr. Griffin, who looks eerily like that old actor Morgan Freeman, rolls his eyes as if he'd heard my excuse a million times.

"There's a twenty-point penalty for turning it in late."

Okay. So the highest I can make is a low B. I sigh. At least it still beats the hell out of an F.

More students begin to drift into the classroom as I return to my desk. Out of curiosity, I glance back out of the window. Tyler and Romeo are gone. I'm unsure how I feel about this whole situation. Should I confront Tyler or wait to see if she comes clean?

I'm still thinking this over when Romeo's boy Chris Hunter comes into the room.

A few of the girls giggle when he strolls in. On the cute scale, Chris easily comes in second under Romeo and, judging by his swagger, he knows this.

Frankly, I still think he's a jerk. After making fun of

my clothes last week, he is permanently number one on my shit list. What's worse is that he actually sits next to me. So for the next forty-five minutes, I have to pretend to ignore him. It isn't easy to do, since he seems to go out of his way to annoy me.

Yesterday, he spent half the time throwing spitballs at my algebra book. How mature is that?

"Pssst. L'il ma?" he whispers. "Did you do the assignment last night?"

I roll my eyes and continue to ignore him.

"Aww. All right. You gonna do me like that, huh?" He slumps back in his chair. "All right. Fine. Be that way."

Mr. Griffin walks up to the board and starts randomly scribbling problems onto it. Everyone pulls out their pencils and starts copying down the problems. I exhale and wonder for the umpteenth time whose bright idea it was to mix the alphabet with numbers. I mean is it a math class or an English class? And why in the hell do we need to know all this stuff?

"Pssst! L'il ma. You got a pencil I can borrow?"

I roll my eyes again. *Who in the hell comes to class without a pencil?*

"Pssst! L'il ma!"

"You can borrow one of my pencils, Chris." Amy, a Red Bone wannabe who sits in front of him, offers.

"Thanks." Chris accepts the pencil, smiling.

Amy's smug gaze cuts toward me, and I definitely let it show that I'm unimpressed with her flirting with Mr. Hot Shot. What? Am I supposed to be jealous or something? Whoopydamndoo.

"Pssst! L'il ma, you got a piece of paper I can borrow?"

"What the hell?" I turn toward him. "Do I have *school supplies* stamped on my forehead?"

He smiles. "I don't know. Lean close and let me see."

I glare at him. "Not funny."

"Does that mean you're going to loan me the paper or not?"

"Fine," I hiss, quickly ripping out two sheets of paper from my notebook and handing it over. Anything to shut him the hell up.

"Thanks," he says, grinning. "I knew that I would wear you down sooner or later."

I go back to thinking about Tyler and Romeo. Are they dating now? What's going to happen when Phoenix finds out? And she's definitely going to find out. Will there be a revolt—a major fight between the BFFs and the Red Bones? Heck, maybe that's why Tyler kissed him in front of everybody. To piss Phoenix off. Actually, that makes the most sense. She didn't kiss Romeo because she wanted him; she kissed him to start a fight. That has to be it. I actually sigh in relief. Tyler didn't go back on her word, she was just being Tyler.

Snap!

I glance over at Chris. In his hand, his pencil was broken in two. He looks me dead in my eye with a sheepish smile.

"Hey, l'il ma. You got a pencil?"

This boy is *really* getting on my nerves. I shake my head and go back to my program of ignoring him. But there's not a minute that ticks by that I don't feel his gaze on me. And I think I kind of like it.

chapter 26

Anjenai—It's A Wrap!

she knows. Why did I lie to her? When I replay the scene at the lunch table today in my head, I try my best to dismiss the way Tyler's eyes blazed through me while she grilled me about Romeo.

Why did I lie?

The question swirls inside my head until I feel dizzy. I've never lied to Kierra and Tyler. Never. And now because of that stupid pact we made, I've backed myself into a corner when all I want to do is scream from the school's rooftop that I'm actually dating the most popular boy in school.

Me. I still can't believe it.

The last three evenings Romeo and I have done about as much kissing as we have been practicing for my basketball tryouts. I don't know how much longer we can keep it a secret; I'm not even sure if I want to. First, I have to figure out a way to break the news to Kierra and Tyler and pray that it doesn't end our friendship.

It shouldn't, I try to reason. We've been through so much, surely this wouldn't come between us. They'll be happy for me, right? I mean, it was a silly pact.

Right?

The last bell of the day rings, and I jump out my seat like everyone else and file out of Mr. Carson's class. It's time for the *big* basketball tryouts. I'm a basket case trying to remember all the basics Romeo had drilled into my head. I'm so lost in my thoughts that I don't see him run up next to me.

"Nervous?" he asks.

I jump with a startled gasp, but then quickly flash him a smile.

"I'm going to take that as a *yes.*"

"Just a little," I confess at his smiling gaze, but already I feel a sense of calm just having him around.

Romeo glances around. "Hey, look. After tryouts, we need to talk."

That doesn't sound too good. "Oh, all right." My calm shatters. Is my wonderful week about to crash to an end? My fear must show on my face because he gives me another beautiful smile.

"Don't worry. You'll do fine. Just remember what I taught you." He winks and then offers me a fist bump for encouragement.

I love it when he does that.

"See you in the gym," he says and takes off.

I expel a long breath and realize I'm trembling—in

part because of the tryouts and part because I have to face Tyler again. She's on to me, and I know it. Should I just confess and get this whole thing over with? What if she blows up—like she always does?

In the girls' locker room, I quickly change into my workout clothes. Glancing around, I try to spot Tyler. Maybe if I just talk to her first—apologize for getting caught up.

"Nah-uh, girl it's true," a voice floats out to me from a group of girls at the end of my row. "I heard Bianca and Raven talking about it in art class. Romeo has a new girlfriend."

My heart stops. Do people already know about us?

"Shut up, girl," a different voice says. "Who is it? I'll tear this bitch's eyes out."

"A chick from Oak Hills. Can you believe it?"

I groan and plop down on the bench.

"Bianca and Raven actually caught them kissing outside during lunch today," the informer continues.

I frown. I wasn't kissing Romeo outside during lunch. What are they talking about?

"Which one?" the chick asks.

"The one that broke Billie Grant's nose," the girl continues. "Tyler Jamison."

"What?" I shout. Surely I heard her wrong. *Romeo is my boyfriend.*

The girl's wide eyes shift to my astonished face. "Humph! Like *you* don't know," one of the nameless chicks utter. "Aren't you like her best friend or something?"

"If you are," the other girl says, "you better warn

Tyler to back off. Phoenix was out sick today but when she finds out, she's going to hit the roof."

"Shh. Here she comes."

Sure enough, Tyler strolls into the locker room and the gossiping girls scramble.

I'm still sitting on the bench, stunned.

Tyler marches down the aisle toward her locker, passing me. In fact, she ignores me, if truth be told. Have I completely misread her? She hadn't caught me lying. *She* was the liar.

I can't stop staring and hearing the gossiping girls over and over in my mind. Tyler and Romeo, kissing.

Kissing!

"*After tryouts, we need to talk,*" he had said. Talk. Is he planning to break up with me—for Tyler?

I feel sick. Please, God, say it's some kind of mistake. A joke. Tyler doesn't kiss boys. She punches them. Everybody knows that.

Nicole breezes into the locker room. "Ohmigod. Ohmigod. I'm so nervous." She smiles at us, oblivious to thickening tension between Tyler and I. "Hello, Tyler—Anjenai. Are you two ready to try out?" she asks, plopping her book bag down and fiddling with the combination on her locker.

I can't bring myself to say anything. I'm still staring at Tyler, waiting for her to look at me.

Tyler and Romeo?

My Romeo.

Kissing!

Nicole glances over her shoulder and back at me.

"You're awfully quiet. Cat got your tongue?" Her gaze shifts to Tyler. "Hey, Ty. You're kinda quiet, too."

"Hey," Tyler mumbles, slamming her locker and proceeding to strip out of her clothes.

Tyler and Romeo.

Kissing?

"What's up with you two?" Nicole asks, finally picking up on our vibe.

"Nothing," Tyler lies.

I still don't say anything. My astonishment is slowly turning into anger. This can't be happening. My own best friend stabs me in the back?

"Alrighty, then," Nicole says. "I'll go get changed." She heads off to one of the bathroom stalls. Apparently she isn't comfortable with getting undressed in front of everyone.

I keep watching Tyler as she undresses, mentally willing her to look my way. It takes a while, but it finally pays off. She stops when she sees the pure hatred written on my face.

It isn't necessary for us to vocalize anything; we both know we're on to each other.

"How in the hell you're just going to straight play me?" I ask, leaping onto my feet, my hands on my hips.

"Play you?" She has the nerve to laugh. "You played yourself, Anje."

I resist the urge to slap her. But just barely. "How long, Tyler?"

"I'm not having this conversation with you," she says, putting on her white cotton tee and then stepping toward the door.

I block her path. "Oh, we're having this conversation," I tell her. She's obviously forgotten that I'm one of the few people not afraid of her.

"What? You're going to fight me for him? Is that it?" Tyler laughs. "Please. I have better things to do with my time."

A crowd slowly gathers.

"You knew I was seeing him. I could tell today at lunch. You knew and then you ran after him to try and take him for yourself!" I'm literally vibrating with anger. With friends like Tyler, I don't need any enemies.

"You knew I liked him first," Tyler charges back.

"First? We saw him at the same time in the principal's office," I try to reason with her insane excuse.

"He tried to *talk* to me first!" she yells.

"And you treated him like shit!" I quickly remind her.

Tyler steps closer to me and lowers her voice to a growling threat. "We made a deal."

"So you kiss him in front of the whole damn school?"

"At least I didn't make out with him in a car like you did in front of the whole damn apartment complex the other night."

The crowd gasps.

"You *saw* that?" My face heats.

"It was kind of hard to miss. Maybe next time you two should just get a room.

"I was taking the garbage out and spotted a lying rat. I've been waiting for two days for you to come clean, but *no*. You just kept telling one lie after another to cover your ass."

The ensuing whispering sounds like bees buzzing.

"So you decide to punish me by trying to steal him for yourself? Is that it?"

She just glares at me.

"I didn't tell you because I didn't want you flying off the handle—like you *always* do."

"Liar. You didn't tell us because you didn't want to look like the *ho* you are."

I step even closer. "You're a bitch. You know that?"

More gasps.

More bees buzzing.

"You were deliberately trying to hurt me."

"Whatever. This friendship is a wrap," Tyler says, trying to move around me.

But I move and bump her shoulder hard.

She spins and crashes into a row of lockers.

Our spectators gasp.

"Oh, what? You're ready to fight me now?" Tyler springs up onto her feet.

"Why not? You're always wanting to fight everyone else. C'mon, you can fight me then!"

"Fight!" a sideline chicks barks.

"Fight! Fight!" everyone begins to chant.

"What's going on?" Nicole shoves her way through the crowd and then plants herself between me and Tyler. Apparently she doesn't know that's a dangerous spot to be in. "You girls are supposed to be best friends, remember? Whatever this is about, it's not worth losing your friendship over."

"Fight! Fight!"

"What's going on in here?" Coach Whittaker thunders, and she rushes into the locker room. The crowd parts like the Red Sea. "Okay, everybody, downstairs," she commands.

Everyone groans.

"Now!" the coach barks and the crowd disperses.

Everyone files out the locker room except the three of us.

"You know what?" I finally say to Tyler. "I don't need friends like you," I spit. I grab the gold B chain around my neck and snatch it off and throw it at Tyler's feet. "No wonder your mother left you. You're not worth sticking around for."

chapter 27

Kierra—The Other Hot Boy

okay. I don't know what the hell is going on with my girls. I hear some rumblings about a fight in the girls' locker room, but before I can check what's going on for myself, the girls start spilling out and saying no one is allowed back in per Coach Whittaker's orders.

Assistant Coach Smith starts directing the girls to run laps around the court to warm up. I return to the stands so I can cheer on my girls. When I sit down and search through the running girls, I don't see Anje and Tyler or even Nicole for that matter.

After a few more minutes pass, I frown and wonder if the girls have changed their minds about trying out. I wish they would have told me. I'll have to ride the public bus by myself to get back home. A few more people filter into the gym and onto the stands to watch the tryouts. To my great shock, Romeo and his two best pals are a part of the crowd.

I straighten in my seat. *Act cool. Pretend you don't see them.*

My gaze returns to the running girls while the assistant coach rolls out a double rack of basketballs. Finally from the side of the stands, I see Anje rush out from the girls' locker room and then join the running girls.

"All right, Anje!" I leap to my feet and clap to let her know I'm here to cheer her on. She doesn't even look up. I plop back down on my seat and continue to clap and cheer even if it is for a couple of laps around the gym.

"Well, well. What do we have here?" Chris asks, not bothering to mask the sarcastic amusement in his voice.

I roll my eyes and flash him a bird.

The boys chuckle.

"Hey, li'l ma. What? You're going to ignore me now?"

"If it'll make you disappear," I say without glancing over my shoulder and pretend I'm spellbound by the wannabe basketball players running in circles.

Nicole and Tyler finally come out of the locker room with Coach Whittaker right behind them. What the hell is going on?

They quickly join the other girls, and I shoot back onto my feet and applaud their appearance.

"Ah. Aren't you the great li'l cheerleader?" Chris comments, still trying to catch my attention. I just switch my weight from one foot to the other, hoping he gets a good look at how I fill out my jeans.

"Mmm. Mmm. Mmm. Li'l ma got a tight frame on her, too," Chris praises.

I try like hell not to smile as I sit back down in my

seat. Chris leans so close that his chin is practically on my shoulder.

"You smell good, too." He inhales.

"And you need a Tic Tac," I lie.

He laughs.

"Seriously," I add and then smile when he pulls back to check his breath. When his chin returns to hover above my shoulder, I smell a fresh stick of spearmint gum.

"Why are you playing so hard to get, girl? You know I'm tryin' to holler at you," he whispers. His lips are so close, they are literally bumping against my lower earlobe.

I just laugh, and I barely pay attention to what's happening on the floor.

"You got a boyfriend, li'l ma?"

"The name is Kierra," I tell him, glancing over my shoulder so that for a brief moment our lips are just millimeters apart. "Use it."

"Kierra," he repeats. "That's nice. So you have a boyfriend...*Kierra?*"

"Why do you want to know?"

"I'd think that's pretty obvious." He asks, flipping a lock of hair off my shoulder, "Are you going to the varsity football game tomorrow night?"

I shrug. Since I'm on the freshman cheerleading squad, I don't cheer at the varsity games. Not that I'm ready. "I don't know."

"Why not? I could use my own personal cheerleader."

I roll my eyes at his little retarded ass. "Then why don't you take your momma to the game?"

Shadiq and Romeo crack up.

"Funny." Chris smiles and winks at me. "Why don't you come over to my man Shadiq's party afterward?"

"A party?" I perk up. My *first* high school party. Is he actually asking me out? "What kind of party?"

"A celebration party. What else? We're going to kick Wheeler's ass tomorrow night."

"What if you lose the game?"

"We won't," he says, his smile growing cocky by the second, but I'm noticing for the first time how his light brown eyes sparkle. I still can't believe that he's trying to holler at me.

The BFFs may have made a pact about Romeo but we didn't say anything about his friends.

"So what's up, Kierra? Are you going to roll with me, or are you going sit here and try to make a brother beg?"

I arch my brows. "I don't know. I might like to see you beg."

His smile widens as he meets my gaze. "I *don't* beg."

I stare him down, determined to look unimpressed.

At long last, he laughs. "I guess there's always a first time for everything," he says. "Please come to the party."

I can't help but laugh now. "Boy, you're a fool."

When our laughter finally dies, he asks again, "So are you coming or what?"

"All right," I say. "We'll roll through with you. Me and my girls, right?"

"Sure. You can bring them. You just make sure you show up."

Chris looks up. "Whoa! Looks like we got a catfight."

I turn around toward the basketball court and see Tyler on her back and Anje glaring down at her. "What did I miss?" Instead of Anje offering a hand to help Tyler up, I'm stunned to see her turn away from her and go back to dribbling her ball.

"What the hell?"

"Looks like there's some bad blood between your girls," Chris says.

Tyler and Anje now have my full undivided attention. I watch as the girls go from practice jump shots to blocking techniques. The whole time, it seems Tyler and Anjenai go out of their way to stay away from each other. On the few times that they don't, it looks like they're seconds from killing each other. What the hell is that all about? I've never seen them like this before.

"This is not good." Maybe Anje found out about the kiss. I glance back at Romeo and try to read his expression but couldn't.

No surprise. Nicole is struggling. She made none of her jump shots, her sparring partner always stole the ball and she looks like she's ready to pass out from the constant running. Poor girl.

My heart goes out to her. There has to be something she's good at.

Anje and Tyler, on the other hand, are amazing—despite trying to kill each other. Anje makes every shot while Tyler only misses one.

"We're watching the makings of a coupla superstars," Chris says next to me.

I bob my head. "Those are my girls!" I clap and

whistle. "Go, Anje! Go, Tyler!" and a little belatedly. "Go, Nicole!"

A few people snicker at the last cheer, and I have to fight back my impulse to cuss them out.

"Nicole needs to give it up," Chris says.

"Shut your mouth," I snap. "At least she's trying."

He holds up his hands. "I didn't know you were that sensitive for the girl."

"She's my friend. I don't appreciate people laughing at her. Didn't your momma teach you that if you don't have nothing nice to say then don't say anything at all?"

Chris mimics zipping his lips and tosses away the key. I smile. "Thank you."

"I like it when you smile at me. You should do it more often," he says.

"If you try to be nice more often then maybe I will."

An hour later, practice finally draws to an end, and I jump up and run down onto the court to finally find out what's going on between my two best friends.

Though the coach makes it clear the list of who made it won't be posted until next week, I'm pretty certain both Tyler and Anje made the cut.

I made it over to Tyler but Anje apparently has a rocket launcher on the heels of her sneakers because she's off the court in record time. "Good job!" I pat Tyler on the back. "You're a shoo-in."

She grunts.

"And guess what? We've been invited to our first high school party!"

I wait for her to be excited, but it's clear I have a long

wait ahead of me. "Oookay. Out with it. What the hell is going on with you and Anje?"

"Fuck, Anjenai! I don't want to hear her name ever again."

She storms off and leaves me and Nicole standing there, looking like idiots. "What the hell was all that about?"

"You'll never believe it," Nicole says and immediately launches into what happened earlier in the locker room. It's enough to make my head spin.

So far this whole high school thing sucks.

chapter 28

Phoenix—There Goes My Baby

"what do you mean they were kissing?" I ask, glaring at Bianca and Raven at the foot of my bed. I stay home sick for one day and this shit happens?

"You should have seen them," Bianca's high baby-soft voice grows so high it actually squeaks. "They were all hugged up behind this bush. I couldn't believe my eyes at first."

I jump from bed and race to the adjoining bathroom. I drop to my knees and dry heave into the toilet. *This can't be happening. This can't be happening.*

"Oh my," Raven says from the bathroom door. "You really are sick."

I remain on my knees hugging the toilet. Tears burn my eyes and try to escape, but I stop them in the nick of time. How could he do this? I'm going to be a laughingstock

at school when everyone learns he left me for that...
backward hood rat, Tyler Jamison.

I don't get it. What the hell does she have that I don't
have?

"Please. I say it's time we teach these girls a lesson,"
Raven vents. "For the past two weeks they have been
nothing but pains in our asses. Taking our tables, taking
our men. What's next?"

"But do what?" Bianca asks. "They already broke one
girl's nose," she says, touching her own. "A broken nose
is *not* cute."

"Okay. Maybe not fight-fight, but we've got to do
something," Bianca reasons. "We've tried spreading
rumors, but people actually like them because of what
they did to Billie and *us*. Last year, we were the most
popular girls in the school. Now that position is being
threatened. We can't just let that shit go. Maybe if we say
they all have some kind of STD or something. Make it
so no guy would ever step to them."

"Yeah and then after that, that Tyler chick beats us up.
That girl has anger-management issues. I thought Billie
Grant was bad," Raven says. "People aren't going to
want to spread rumors about those girls because they fear
that Tyler."

"With good reason," I add. "She's always ready to
fight on the drop of a dime." I climb onto my feet and
walk over to the sink to splash water on my face. Patting
my face dry, I glance into the mirror and think about my
ex. I can't lose him. We've been together for so long.

I love him.

And he loves me. He's told me so a thousand times.

I almost break down in front of my girls and start crying, but that would be a mistake. Bianca and Raven were my best friends, but I know they are just looking for any signs of weakness. Loyal, they're not.

I draw a deep breath and take in my reflection in the mirror. Despite my nausea, I know I still look better than Tyler Jamison—or any other girl at that school.

"It's okay, girls. I'll get him back," I promise them as well as myself. I turn and face them. "This is war."

"All right," Raven says, smiling.

"Maybe a good time to talk with him is at Shadiq's party tomorrow night," Bianca suggests.

"Party?" I ask. "What party?"

"You didn't know about the party?" Bianca asks.

I didn't, but I'm not about to let them know that. "Oh, that party." I wave them off. "I've been so sick today that I forgot."

"You'll be all right in time for the game tomorrow night, right?"

"Oh, for sure. And you're right. The party will be the perfect place to confront Romeo." I give them a confident smile, but inside I'm dying. I have to get Romeo back. I just have to. There's no way I'm having this baby without him.

chapter 29

Nicole—Unwanted

I hate my life, I keep chanting inside my head as I storm into my house. I totally sucked at basketball tryouts. I can't even run and dribble a ball at the same time. There's not a chance in hell I made it onto the team. Tears burn my eyes as I slam the door behind me. I make a beeline toward the kitchen.

"Nicole, is that you?" Mom yells out.

"Yeah, it's me," I answer, rolling my eyes. I wonder if she even bothered to get out of bed today. Mom always sinks into a deep depression whenever she breaks up with a guy. Her pity party consists of ice cream, pickles and cigarettes. It's very weird.

The last rich guy promised to take mom away from all this. Give her a ring and set up in a house as big as the one my dad lives in. Now that our plans of leaving a life of mediocrity has fallen through, she'll spend the next six months in bed, glued to her soap opera.

No wonder I'm pathetic. It's in the genes.

I grab a frozen pizza out of the freezer and preheat the oven to four-fifty. I know the last thing I need is to eat a whole pizza, but I need something to cheer me up after the disastrous day I had. I grab the two-liter root beer bottle and the carton of vanilla ice cream. If I'm going to break my new diet, I might as well go all out.

Of course I wouldn't need any of this stuff if I was anywhere near perfect like my half sister, Phoenix. Everyone thinks *she's* beautiful.

It's not fair. Nothing is fair for a bastard daughter of a multimillionaire. Is it too much to ask that every once in a while *I* get some fabulous clothes, a decent car or my own credit card? Doesn't his blood run through my veins just like Phoenix?

Of course it would also be nice if my mother finally lands a husband instead of a sugar daddy all the time. I give myself an extra scoop of vanilla ice cream and don't rule out the possibility of coming back for more later.

The oven beeps, letting me know that it's time to put the pizza in. Afterward, I take my root beer float and shuffle my way into the living room. I spend about as much time in here alone as I do my own bedroom. I plop down on the sofa, grab the remote and quickly search to see whether *106 & Park* is on yet.

I reach the channel just when the crowd is going wild. A few minutes later, my favorite rapper Lil Jon struts out, and I start bouncing on the sofa. The veejay, Rosci, is greeted with a kiss on the cheek, and I'm instantly jealous. She's tall and skinny, too. Maybe when I finally lose this weight, I'll be able to get a boyfriend.

Everybody else seems to have a boyfriend. Hell, at this point I'd be happy with one of those science nerds with thick glasses and an acne problem just so I can have someone to stroll with me to my locker or walk me to class.

Lil Jon catches my attention again and I smile. He's my fantasy boyfriend. His long dreads, tattoos and thug style is just off the chain. Rocsi's small ass is flirting up a storm and irritating me.

I jump off the sofa and race back into the kitchen to grab a bag of Cheetos. I return in time to see Lil Jon introduce his latest video. "Aww. This my jam!" I close my eyes and start shaking my hips to the beat. In my mind, there's a skinnier version of me dancing with Lil Jon. Everyone from school is there, whispering, pointing and wishing they were me.

"What on earth are you doing?"

I freeze and glance over at the living room arch to see my mother in her blue silk robe, frowning at me. "Nothing. I was just dancing," I say, my face hot with embarrassment.

"You look like you were having an epileptic fit," she tells me and then shuffles off into the kitchen.

I roll my eyes and return to the sofa, feeling disgusted with myself.

"You're having pizza, *again?*" my moms asks. "What's wrong with these Lean Cuisine you begged me to buy? I thought you said you were going on a diet?"

Here we go again.

"I don't know why you always have me wasting my money on this stuff. You keep telling me that you want to lose weight, but you keep eating food like it's going out of style."

I roll my eyes.

"Does your book bag belong on this counter?"

"No, ma'am." I get up and go to the kitchen to get my stuff.

At the sink, Mom is lighting up a cigarette. She's the only person in the world I know who only smokes hanging over the kitchen sink and tapping ashes down the drain. For a brief moment, I glance over her slim figure and wonder why I didn't inherit her metabolism. No matter what she eats, she stays slim.

She looks at me dispassionately. "Did you learn anything at school today?" she asks, her words slur.

I guess that means that she's been drinking.

I don't answer. I just grab my bag and return to the living room. Unfortunately, my mother follows behind me.

"You're eating Cheetos, too...and a root-beer float? My God, Nicole. You keep this up and I'll have to scrape up money to send you to fat camp."

"Thanks for the encouragement," I mumble.

"Don't give me that," she sasses with her hands on her hips. "I always encourage you. You just don't listen."

Tears are starting to well as I glare at the television. Lil Jon has lost all effect on me. For a few long seconds, neither one of us says anything. When she finally finishes glaring a hole into my head, she tells me, "*Your father* called today."

I glance up at her. Suddenly her bitter behavior makes sense: her tear-stained face, her unkempt hair and the alcohol.

"He says that he wants you to come out and stay with him this weekend."

I roll my eyes. "I don't want to go."

My response gives my mom her first genuine smile. She loves the fact that I don't like my father.

"I told him that, but you're going to have to go anyway. It's the only way I can get him to pay the rent. He spends time with you and I get a check."

Lucky me. I weigh whether I should protest again, but what's the point? She's going to make me go anyway, which also means when he shows up there'll be another fight between the two of them. They might even land up in bed together. That's usually how it works.

He'll show up, and Mom will be wearing her best clothes and her hair and makeup will be flawless. I'll put my bags in the car and then wait until they either finish fighting or having sex before being driven to Phoenix's house. At one time, I think my mom really did love my dad. I wish I could say the same for him.

Once at his house, my stepmother and sister will treat me like shit for even being born for a couple of weeks. I'm a reminder of his infidelity. Sometimes I think that's *exactly* why he wants me there. The bottom line is my father is a mean bastard. And he gets off on it. He loves keeping my mom and his wife down.

The person that is the absolute apple of his eye is Phoenix. *She* can do no wrong. He lavishes money and gifts on her. Then again, maybe that's his way of being mean toward me. His always buying her things in front of me, constantly reminding me of my place in life.

God, I hate my life. How much longer until that pizza is done?

chapter 30

Tyler—I Get So Lonely.

"NO wonder your mother left you. You're not worth sticking around for."

I can't believe Anje said that to me. Every time I think about it I just want to...cry. Is she right? Is it my fault that everyone leaves me? Am I so unlovable?

I think about the kiss I shared with Romeo and then the humiliation of him telling me that he wants Anje over me. What the hell was I thinking? Or maybe I wasn't. Maybe that joint was stronger than I thought. I chuckle and think about the dime bag I bought and stuffed in my top drawer. A hit would be nice now so I can just forget about this.

I'm trying to act like it doesn't hurt, but it does.

Big-time.

For the first time in my life, I'm angry at the person who I normally run to when I'm in pain. I should've opened up and told Anje why I kissed Romeo. I was jealous. She has what I want...or who I want.

What Anje said was true. I deliberately set out to hurt her. I deliberately tried to steal her new boyfriend. I frown, thinking about that. It's actually pretty messed up. I'm messed up. My tears swell.

Why would I do that?

"Hey, baby girl." My dad peeks inside my bedroom.

"Daaad!" I pull the covers up over my head. "You're supposed to knock first."

"I'm sorry, but isn't it time for you to get up? You're going to be late for school."

"I'm not going," I mumble and roll over.

"What—are you sick or something?" He walks over to the bed and sits down on the edge. "What are your symptoms?"

Why can't he just leave me alone? Maybe go hook up with Kierra's sister like I know he wants to. "I don't know. An upset stomach, I guess."

"No fever?" He reaches over and places his hand against my forehead.

"Dad, please. Go away."

"What? I'm just trying to check on you. It's not like you get sick often," he says.

By the tone of his voice, I can tell I've hurt him. Even though I know he's trying, I just want to be left alone. I roll away and wait for him to take the hint.

He doesn't.

"Is there something you want to talk about?" he asks. "Something bothering you?"

Since when do we talk? "No," I lie.

He draws several deep breaths, while staying on the edge of my bed. "Dad, I just don't feel like going to school. Missing one day isn't a big deal."

The room is silent for a moment and then he says, "All right. I guess I better get going. I have to work today whether *I* feel like it or not."

I roll my eyes at his attempt to make me feel guilty. The bed rises when he stands up, and I listen as he walks back over to the door. But then he stops. I almost moan out loud.

"Baby girl, you'd come to me if you really had a problem, wouldn't you?" he asks.

I don't say anything. My only other option is to lie.

"All right then, baby. I hope you feel better." At last he turns and walks out of my room.

I pull the covers from my head and then cry quietly into my pillow.

chapter 31

Anjenai—The End of the Road

"**Anje,** you haven't touched your breakfast."

I blink and then glance up at Granny. "What?"

"Your breakfast," she says. "You haven't touched it."

"Oh." I stab my fork back into my scrambled eggs and take a bite to appease her.

She just frowns at me. "Baby, is something wrong?"

"Hmm? Uh, no, ma'am."

"She lying," Hosea and Edafe chime in, panting.

"She was crying all night," Edafe tattles. "I heard her."

"Shut up," I hiss at him and resist the temptation to make my point by kicking him in the shins.

Granny pulls up a chair and takes a seat. "Anje, why were you crying last night?"

"No reason," I lie. "It's not a big deal."

"It must be a big deal if you're willing to lie about it," she says, taking a seat at the table.

Great. Everyone is calling me a liar now.

Granny's large brown eyes land on me like she's reading me like a book. "Come on, baby. Tell me what's wrong. Is someone giving you trouble at school?"

At this point I wish it was that simple. Granny waits patiently even though I don't want to burden her with my troubles. She has enough on her plate. She's run out of her diabetic medicine and doesn't know how she's going to get the money to get her refills.

"C'mon, baby. We're family. We're supposed to be here for one another."

"It's about the BFFs," I confess.

"What? Kierra and Tyler?"

"Yes, ma'am," I say dejectedly, staring down at my plate. My vision blurs through my tears. "See. We all like the same boy at school," I begin.

"Oooh, Anjenai has a boyfriend," the twins chant.

"Shut up," I snap, again resisting kicking both of them.

"Now, you boys stop teasing your sister and finish your breakfast," Granny reprimands with a face that says she means business. The boys quiet down, but their wide grins mean their teasing will continue at another time.

Granny returns her attention to me. "Now, go on, baby. Finish your story."

"Well, like I said, we all like the same boy, so we decided to make a pact that in this situation we should all back off. You follow me?"

"Umm. Hmm," she says, patiently waiting but eyebrows furrowing close together. "Now is this the same boy that was helping you learn basketball this week?"

"Yes, ma'am."

"The one that you're outside kissing way past your curfew the past few nights?"

I gasp. "You saw that?"

"Honey, everybody saw," Granny says with a soft laugh. "I'm proud that there was only kissing going on." She eyes me. "It's just been kissing, right?"

"Right," I say, dropping my head in embarrassment.

My brothers snicker and start making kissing noises.

"Boys!" Granny warns.

They fall silent again.

I stare at my scrambled eggs. "Tyler also saw us out there. She waited to see whether I was going to tell her and Kierra about me and Romeo. When I didn't, she blew up and then tried to steal him from me by kissing him in front of the whole school."

Granny drew back. "Humph. Sure does sound like a whole lot of kissing going on."

I lift my head. "She *knew* about us, and she purposely set out to take him from me. What kind of friend does that?" When Granny doesn't answer, I shrug. "So anyway. We got into a big fight, and now we're not friends anymore."

"Oh, baby." Granny reaches across the table and squeezes my hand. "Well, I'm not gonna lie and say that this isn't a sticky situation," she says. "But both of you were wrong. But you girls have been through so much over the years, I don't believe for a minute that you girls can just up and stop caring for one another over something this silly. You're just hurt right now."

Tears slide down my face. "I'm not sorry that I like

him, Granny. I wasn't trying to be malicious. I just didn't know how to tell them. But I would never do what Tyler did to me. Never."

"I know, baby. But this is all a part of growing up. You still love Tyler or you wouldn't have been crying all night, and if you girls still love each other then this can be fixed. Trust me on this, baby. Just talk to her."

"Tyler doesn't know how to talk. She just knows how to punch."

"You and Kierra know why better than anyone," Granny reminds me. "She doesn't fight because she thinks she's tough. It's because she hurt."

"I know." But I continue to shake my head. "I can't see us getting past this any time soon. But we'll see," I say, wiping my face. "I better get going or I'm going to miss the bus."

"All right, baby." She leans over and kisses me on the cheek. "Try to cheer up."

"Thanks, Granny."

I grab my jacket and backpack and race out the door. While I'm standing at the bus stop, my stomach is tangled into knots waiting for Tyler to show up. Do I try to talk to her, or do I just ignore her?

How is Kierra going to treat me?

No sooner does her name cross my mind, when I see Kierra heading toward me. I'm so nervous about what is about to go down that I'm literally shaking like a leaf, but I stand and wait and pray for the best.

chapter 32

Kierra—Long Road to Hoe

I've been thinking about this moment all night, wondering what the heck I'm going to say when I see Anjenai again. To be honest, I'm not tripping over the fact that she's been seeing Romeo behind our backs. I'm more stunned about what went down between her and Tyler than anything.

I want to get Tyler's side of the story, but she's made it clear that she's not talking to either one of us—even though I didn't do anything. Typical Tyler. She'll have to blow off a little steam first, but then she'll calm down. At least I hope. It's sad that the very thing that we were trying to prevent happened anyway. Somehow we have to come back together and bridge our differences. I just hope that it's sooner and not later.

"Whatsup?" I ask Anje when I finally arrive at the bus stop. Maybe we should just fake it.

She shrugs. "Nothing much. You?"

I shake my head and sigh. "Tyler's not coming to school today. Her dad says she's sick."

Anje rolls her eyes and turns her head.

"Hey, look. Give her some time."

"I'm not sure I want to give her time. I'm not sure that I want to fix this," Anje explodes. It's shocking since she's supposed to be the calm one.

"C'mon, Anje. You both were wrong."

"It's the *intent*. I didn't set out to get Romeo. He was just helping me to prepare for basketball tryouts…and one thing led to another. And when it happened I didn't know what to do or how to tell you guys after that stupid pact."

"Not saying anything is like lying. You lied. That's probably what set her off," I tell her. "We both know Tyler has trouble expressing herself."

"Now that's my fault, too? Tyler needs a shrink. You know it, and I know it. If I'd told her what had happened, she still would have blown up. Not telling her doesn't change anything. We'll still have to go through her *I'm not talking to you* routine."

"True." I'm starting to feel like there's no right answer to this situation. We drop the subject when the school bus rolls into view. After we're seated, Anje finally speaks again.

"Do *you* hate me?"

I turn toward her and tell her the truth. "I can *never* hate you, Anjenai. You're my best friend. And knowing Tyler like I do, she doesn't hate you either. She's just mad. She's mad at the whole world. All the time. Something tells me if it wasn't this it was going to be something else."

"I said some hateful things to her," she says. "I wish I could take it back."

"Don't worry. We'll get through this. Tyler will calm down. You'll see." We're quiet again for a moment, and then I have to ask the one thing on my mind. "So are things *real* serious between you and Romeo? I mean, are you like boyfriend and girlfriend now?"

She tries to suppress a smile, but can't. "I like him," she admits, her eyes dancing a bit. "He even asked me to go to tonight's football game."

I light up at this. "Are you also going to Shadiq's after party?"

"Are you going, too?"

"Yeah, Chris invited me. Can you believe it? He was hitting on me all through your tryouts yesterday."

Anje's jaw drops open. "You and Chris Hunter? You guys are always practically at each other's throats."

"What can I say? Love is strange."

"Love?"

I shrug. "Well, at least something similar."

"It's going to be our first high school party," Anje says, smiling.

We look at one another and then erupt into giggles.

Anje and I bounce in our seats, but then just as quickly we calm down. One person is missing in our small celebration, and it feels strange. "Don't worry," I tell her. "I'll get Tyler to come, even if I have to drag her kicking and screaming."

Anje shakes her head. "If she knows I'm going to be there, then you'll probably have to do just that."

chapter 33

Tyler—Traveling Down the Wrong Road

I'm high as a kite and happy that I decided to stay home from school. My two new girlfriends Michelle and Trisha were more than happy to skip with me and hang out at my apartment.

"What time does your dad come home?" Michelle asks.

"Whenever the hell he feels like it," I tell them. "There's no set time."

"Well, damn," Trisha pipes up. "We need to hang out at your crib more often."

Michelle laughs and bobs her head. "Most definitely."

A couple of hours later, I use the money left in the kitchen to order us a pizza and hot wings. When my little dime bag is gone, Trisha pulls out her cell phone and calls Kerosene and a few more friends. Now it's a full-fledged party.

I have to admit these girls are pretty cool to hang out

with. All they do is chill, get high and talk shit about everyone at school. Hell, I'm down with that. Before everybody goes, I know I'm really going to have to spray this place down with Febreeze before my dad comes home.

"So what's this I hear about you kissing that punk Romeo?" Michelle asks. "You feeling him or what?"

I laugh. With this buzz, that whole thing seems like it was so long ago. "That was nothing," I tell them.

"That ain't what I heard," some chick I don't even know says. "I heard he had his tongue all down your throat. Probably trying to make his bourgie-ass girlfriend mad by messing with an Oak Hill girl. You know she'll pop her lid. We ain't good enough for them."

Most of the group bobs their heads. Apparently none of us like the rezoning of our districts.

I, of course, don't tell them that it was me who was kissing Romeo and not the other way around. But that's none of their business.

"Now Phoenix is the one that really need to get her ass whooped," Michelle says. "She's always prancing around that school like the sun rises and sets on her ass, but I hear her father works with like the mob or something."

"The mob?" I say. "What mob is there in Atlanta?"

She shrugs. "I don't know. I'm just repeating what I heard."

"Right." I roll my eyes. "No more weed for you. This shit got you tripping."

"You girls ain't nothing but a bunch of haters," Kerosene says. "Phoenix is fine as hell." A wide grin spreads across his face. "I know I'd do her ass any day of the week."

Kerosene's girlfriend, Adele, leans over and pops him on the back of the head. "Your ass ain't funny," she snaps.

"Whatever." He laughs. "I'm just being real. Phoenix is fine."

"In that case then," she retaliates, "I wouldn't mind doing Romeo or Shadiq."

"Sheeeit." Kerosene takes a deep drag off the joint. "Those motherfuckers ain't shit." He looks up at Adele. "And I better not catch your ass hanging around them."

"Whatever," she says, mimicking him. "I'm just being real."

Clearly Kerosene doesn't care for it, and he takes the bait. "All right. Don't play me like that. We ain't always going to be in front of your friends."

I just laugh at their silly asses.

"Yo, Tyler. Where's your bathroom at?"

I look at this girl. Stella, I think her name is. "Straight down the hall," I tell her.

"Don't drop nothing that don't flush," Kerosene shouts.

"Eww." We all make faces, and Adele pops him on the head again.

"Hey. Stop the violence."

"You ain't funny, Kerosene," Stella shouts as she makes her way down the hall.

He just laughs.

The group returns to laughing and talking about nothing. I start attacking the pizza like I haven't eaten in a week. The great thing about this day is that I haven't been thinking about the BFFs that much. And now that I am, the whole thing does seem sort of silly. Big deal, Anje is dating the most popular boy in school. I should have just been happy for her.

The image of our big fight starts to play slowly in my mind. Still, that bit about people leaving me stings, but didn't I deserve it?

"Oh, God. I gotta pee," I say suddenly.

The girls sitting next to me laugh.

"Shut up," I tell them and force myself to stand. The room spins and wobbles around a bit.

"Damn, girl. Are you all right?"

I wave them off and try to step over their feet. "Y'all don't break nothing while I'm gone," I warn. "I don't want to have to kick somebody's ass."

They all laugh, but I mean it.

As I approach the bathroom something nudges me at the back of my mind. Did somebody say that they had to go to the bathroom? Then why was it empty? I move away from the bathroom and move farther down the hall. When I reach my father's room, I see Stella.

"What are you doing in here?" I snap.

Stella jumps. In her hands I see my mom's old jewelry box.

"What are you doing with that?" I challenge, stepping into my father's room. My buzz is gone, and my anger is roaring back to the surface.

Stella puts the box down. "Nothing. I was just looking around."

"Looking around? Bitch, this ain't your house!"

"What the hell is going on back there?" Kerosene shouts. I hear people rushing from the living room.

"I'm going to ask you again," I threaten Stella. "What the hell are you doing in here?"

"N-nothing."

"Nothing my ass! You in here stealing from me?"

"N-no."

"Whatcha got in your pockets?" Before she has a chance to answer, I jam my hand into her front jean pocket and pull out a locket. My mother's locket.

"Now wait—"

That's all she gets out before I land a punch across that weak-ass jaw of hers. Before I know it, I'm straight wailing on her ass, popping her in the mouth, eye and every damn where else I can get at.

"Fight! Fight! Fight!"

Trisha pulls out her camera phone and starts recording.

"Fight! Fight! Fight!"

Damn right it's a fight. It feels damn good to be landing these punches, and it takes a long time beating her ass. I don't give a damn about her screaming and hollering. How is she going to come up in my crib and disrespect me like this? Is she crazy?

And not nan-one of her friends jump in to try and help her ass either.

"Get her off. Get her off," Stella screams.

"Aw, shit. Aw, shit." Kerosene laughs. "Tyler going old school on her ass. You getting this shit, Trisha?"

"Hell, yeah. I'm post this shit on YouTube."

"You fuckin' bitch, get the hell up out here!" I scream.

Stella tries to get away, but I'm not making it easy. In the end she ends up crawling out my dad's room. Even then I'm kicking her. "*All* of you get the hell out!"

"Why the hell we got to go?" Michelle complains.

"Get out!"

"Aw, shit. This is foul," Kerosene says.

"GET OUT!"

I herd all their asses toward the front door. "That's right, get your shit and get out."

Everybody moans and groans, but they know I ain't playing. When the last person walks out, I slam the door behind them. Frustrated, I slump down against it and close my eyes. Within seconds, the tears come.

I miss my real friends.

chapter 34

Romeo—Mr. Touchdown

I'm riding high during the first varsity football game of the new season. Sure, a part of it is because our team is up 21-7 and in the fourth quarter, but a lot of it has to do with Anjenai sitting up in the stands cheering me on. In all honesty, I didn't know what would happen after the whole Tyler kissing incident. I didn't want to rat her girl out, but with Raven and Bianca catching us, I had to come clean.

Once I heard about the fight between Anje and Tyler in the girls' locker room, I felt guilty for being the cause of a rift between them. One thing I am grateful for is that she appears to have forgiven me. It's just another reason in a growing list of why I'm truly feeling this girl. She's calm, cool and collected. We've only been together for a few days, but I have a good feeling about all of this. A real good feeling.

No more drama.

Pulled from the fourth quarter, I'm left to watch the last

few minutes of the game from the sidelines. All the while I feel another set of eyes blazing a hole into the side of my head. I don't have to look to know that it's Phoenix watching my every move.

No doubt she knows the deal—or at least part of it. Some are confused to which girl I'm truly dating—Tyler or Anjenai. Either way, I know Phoenix is straight losing it right now. But what's there to say? It's over. It's been over. It's time to move on.

I told my boys about my seeing Anjenai. When they finished laughing it up, they saw I was serious. They can't see what we have in common. I've tried to explain to them that I'm just feeling her. The way she laughs, the way she sees things and her quiet toughness. One thing Chris and Shadiq do like about my new girl is her undeniable skills on the basketball court. Sure I've taught her a couple of plays—how to zig and zag—but the girl is a natural. She's gonna be a star.

To combat Phoenix's evil stare, I turn to the cheering crowd again and see Anjenai waving at me. I wave back and surprise more than a few.

The visiting team, Wheeler High's Wildcats, scores another touchdown on us and suddenly the game is close. Time runs out and the Jackson Eagles win our first game of the football season 21-14.

The crowd goes crazy. And I'm the first to race toward the Gatorade to dump all over our coach.

In the locker room, everyone is buzzing about Shadiq's party. I can't wait to get there with Anjenai on my arm. This is new ground, and I hope she likes my friends. Hell,

I hope they like her. At least Chris has chilled out popping off about Oak Hill girls since he's started feeling Anjenai's girl, Kierra.

"You two are making my life hell," Shadiq complains while we scrub up in the shower. "Raven has been bitchin' about how you played her girl Phoenix. Dawg, she wanted me to tell you not to come to my party."

I just roll my eyes at him. "Are you that damn whipped?"

"Nah. I'm just saying that everything was cool when it was the three of us with the Red Bones. Now I got unnecessary drama."

I laugh. "What did you tell her?"

"I recited the golden rule—bros before hos."

Chris and I crack up. "Damn right," I tell him. "Damn right. Besides, Phoenix played herself," I say and then duck my head under the shower's steady spray.

"Yeah, maybe. But it's all I hear. You slumming it with the Oak Hill hood rats."

"Watch yourself," I warn.

"I'm just repeating what she's saying," Shadiq says. "Don't shoot the messenger."

"What I do is none of Raven or Phoenix's damn business anymore."

"For sure. For sure," Chris readily agrees. "Plus, that girl has all the potential of being Jackson High's first major female star."

"Too much drama is exactly why I left Phoenix's ass alone," I tell him. "Anjenai is calm, cool and uncomplicated. It's just the way I like it."

"Whatever, man. Whatever."

* * *

Shadiq's crib is one of the largest houses in Fulton County. His father, a big-time music producer, currently has eight acts in the top ten on the Billboard chart. Shadiq actually stays in the estate's cottage a few yards from the main house. By the time me and Anjenai arrive, there's a line of cars already parked on the estate.

"Wow. This is Shadiq's house?" she asks from the passenger seat.

"Yeah, pretty cool, huh?" I park the car. I glance over at her wearing my green-and-white football jacket. She looks cute. It's the first time I've seen her wear a little bit of makeup, and I have to admit her purplish lip gloss has me wanting to kiss her every five minutes. When I help her out of the car, she still looks as if we've just arrived to one of the Seven Wonders of the World.

"This place is huge. I bet everyone has their own room here."

I frown. What an odd statement.

"Yo, Romeo. Nice game!" someone calls out.

I wave not really placing the face to a name. This actually happens quite often.

Anjenai looks nervous.

"Are you all right?" I ask, leading her toward the cottage.

"Oh, yeah," she says. "It's just a lot to take in."

I smile. "You'll blend in just fine. You're with me."

The music is bumping, and everyone is gettin' their groove on. To her credit, Anjenai tries to loosen up, but I can tell she's nervous and out of her element. To make her feel comfortable, I drape my arm around her shoulder and pull her close. The way she fits against me, I'm content to hold her just like this.

To say that we are the center of attention and no doubt the subject of every conversation is an understatement. Far as I'm concerned, everybody better just get used to us.

Twenty minutes later, it looks like Shadiq has invited everyone from Jackson High. The party spills out all the way to the pool area, and some idiots are jumping in—clothes and all.

Everyone, it seems, stops to congratulate me on the game and proceeds to make predictions that I'm going to be a star athlete like my father. It takes me a minute to realize that Anjenai is a little uncomfortable with everyone crowding our space.

"Better get you used to it," I tell her. "You'll be getting the star treatment when basketball season starts."

"Yeah, right." She shakes her head.

"Hey, you want to dance?" I ask.

She hesitates.

"What? Don't tell me you need lessons on how to dance, too."

She eases from my side and looks me up and down. "Don't play. My question is can you keep up?"

"Aight then." I smile. "Let's see whatcha workin' with." We head out poolside where everyone is getting their swerve on. The DJ throws on Flo Rida's "Shorty Got Low"—and that's just what my girl does. I'm right up against her, amazed how she flips the script on me again.

"Aw right. My *baby* got skills." I praise. It's the first time I call her that, and I can tell by the way she lights up that she likes it.

From the "Soulja Boy" to "Walk It Out," we're having a blast. And I'm lovin' every minute of it.

chapter 35

Tyler—Swallowing My Pride

I don't know how I let Kierra talk me into coming to this stupid party. But from the moment we arrive, I feel like we've been thrown out of our element. The house is as big as some hotels, and Shadiq's private cottage can easily house a large family.

"What's with your girl? She doesn't speak?" Chris asks Kierra sitting in the passenger seat of his car.

"I can speak for myself," I tell him from the backseat.

His gaze shifts to his rearview mirror, and our eyes clash. "Good to know."

Kierra turns around in her seat and gives me the *will-you-chill* look.

I just roll my eyes. It wasn't my idea to come to this thing. She wants so badly to blend in with these rich kids. Her and Anjenai. Kierra has Chris. Anjenai has Romeo. Who do I have?

Nobody.

As usual.

Two weeks into the school year and I've been reduced to playing the third wheel on an obvious date. I draw a deep breath. Here I go again. I need to get myself together and just chill. When we step out of the car and attempt to migrate toward the heart of the party, it looks to me like every kid in Fulton County has been invited to this thing. That's good for me I suppose. It'll make it easier for me to become invisible.

Kierra finally detaches herself from Chris's side to come back toward me and loop her arm through mine. "C'mon, Tyler. This is a party," she says. "We're here to have a good time."

"Yeah, I guess."

"Hi, Tyler! Kierra! Over here!" We look up to see Nicole waving as she makes her way toward us. "I didn't know you guys were going to be here," she says, smiling.

Nicole scored an invite?

As if hearing the question drift across my head, she answers, "This weekend I'm stayin' with my father, and he of course pawns me off on Phoenix. She dropped me off and went back home to change out of her cheerleading outfit. She always has to stage an entrance."

I turn and look at Kierra. "This night just keeps getting better and better."

Chris invades our small circle and drapes an arm around Kierra's shoulder. "Li'l ma, are we going to go do this or what?"

Kierra glances back at me, and I give her the okay. "Go ahead. I'll be fine."

"Are you sure?" she asks.

"Positive."

"All right," she says and beams a smile before disappearing into the crowd.

"I guess that leaves me and you," Nicole says, shrugging. "The two single chicks."

"Yeah, I guess so." I glance around and notice a few people drinking. "Where is everyone getting the punch?"

"Over by the cottage. C'mon. I'll take you over there."

We walk through a maze of dancing and laughing people and then ladle out a few cups of obviously spiked punch. "Well, this is definitely a party starter." As I glance around, I bob my head to the music.

"So what did you think of the game?" Nicole asks.

"It was all right," I say. "Football is not my thing."

She nods, and we have efficiently ended our list of things to talk about. But by the time we finish our second cup of punch we're more than loosened up and have become quite giggly. I very rarely giggle.

I even manage to get some poor soul who I believe is in my English class to feel sorry for me and ask me to dance. I think his name's James. Anyway, we make it to poolside, the apparent dance floor. That's when I spot Anjenai and Romeo getting their groove on.

I feel that familiar kick of jealousy in the pit of my stomach. I try to look away, but I can't. My dance partner is grooving while I only manage a pathetic two-step. For the most part, I'm just drinking in Romeo's handsome profile. I can tell by the way he's smiling that he's really having a good time.

So is Anjenai.

Why can't I be happy for her?

"Hey, remember me?"

I turn back toward James. "Oh. Sorry." I get back to our dance. I give him the attention he wants for all of thirty seconds before my gaze drifts back to Romeo and Anjenai. But then slowly but surely everyone stops dancing. It's not long before I see why.

Phoenix Wilder has made her grand entrance.

chapter 36

Phoenix—A Woman on a Mission

I'm confused. I thought Romeo was kicking it with that Tyler bitch—not her nerdy sidekick. All eyes are on me as my heart is hammering its way through my chest. Finally, the music stops.

"What the hell, Romeo? Is one broke project ho not enough for you?" I ask.

"Oooh," the surrounding crowd choruses.

"Phoenix, don't this," Romeo warns.

"What the hell did you just call me?" Anjenai challenges, stepping toward me.

I take two steps forward. I'm more than willing to help her with her damn hearing. "I called you a *project ho,*" I repeat.

"Oh no the hell she didn't," another voice charges from my right.

Kierra peels away from Chris's side to make her way

next to her girl. "Bitch, you better back down or get knocked down," she says, swirling her neck like we're at the ghetto Olympics or something.

Bianca and Raven quickly flank my sides.

I look around. "Don't you hood rats usually travel in threes?"

"You're a fine one to talk," Anje spits.

"If it's a third person you need, I'm right here." To my amazement, my own *half* sister steps out of the crowd. The traitor.

"You've got to be kidding me," I say.

"Fight! Fight! Fight!" the crowd chants.

"Whoa. Whoa. Whoa," Romeo shouts across the crowd. "There's not going to be a fight," he says, planting himself between the two groups.

"You damn right!" Shadiq thunders his way through. "This is my damn party. Phoenix, you need to roll your drama queen ass up out of here if you came to start trouble."

"What?" Raven asks. "How are you gonna talk to my girl like that?" she asks.

"Hey, you can hit the road with her," Shadiq says. "This is getting old. DJ, get that damn music back on."

The crowd moans in disappointment but then starts grouping back off to dance. Some continue to ogle us.

Shadiq turns back to me. "I mean it, Phoenix. You gonna have to head out. Everyone was having a good time until you showed up."

"I didn't come here for your damn party," I say. "I came because I have to talk to Romeo."

Romeo shakes his head and drapes an arm possessively around Anjenai. "Sorry, Phoenix. But we ain't got shit to say to one another."

My face heats up. "It's important," I insist. I'm not going out like this. I'm not giving up on him without a fight.

"Then say what you gotta say," Romeo says. "Whatever you have to say to me, you can say in front of my new girl."

I hesitate.

"See, Phoenix. That the main problem with you," Romeo says. "Too much drama."

"Believe me," I tell him, glancing to our few onlookers. "You want to hear this in private."

He gives me a half laugh, rolls his eyes and then starts to walk away.

"Romeo!" I snap. "I mean it. Just give me three minutes of your precious time, and I'll go away."

He stops and looks back over his shoulder. I can see him weighing his options. "Three minutes?" he asks.

"Make it two."

He draws in a deep breath, glances at his girl and says, "I'm sorry, baby. But let me just holler at her for a minute."

Baby? He's calling her baby now?

Anjenai doesn't look happy. Too damn bad.

Finally, she says, "All right. I guess I'll go get a drink."

He nods and then right in front of me he leans forward and kisses her.

"Goddamn," Raven swears. "That's foul."

Tears burn my eyes.

Romeo walks over to me. "Two minutes."

"Let's go somewhere private."

He draws a deep breath and then turns toward the cottage.

I give Anjenai a quick sneer and then follow behind him. Inside, we make our way to the bedroom, kicking out a few people playing touchy-feely in the dark. When they clear out, I lock the door and turn toward Romeo.

"All right, Phoenix. Spit it out."

I'm suddenly nervous.

"Tick tock," he says. "Time's a wasting."

"I want you back," I say bluntly.

He laughs. "Is that it? *That's* what was so important?"

"Romeo—"

"Look, Phoenix. We've been down this road too many times. We get together. We break up. We get together. We break up. It's time to let it go. I mean, I know we've been together since sixth grade and all but that was puppy love. We've changed. We've grown apart. Let's just accept that and move on."

"And you want to move on with that hood—"

"Hey! Watch yourself. I'm not going to sit here and let you talk about my girl. I'm feeling Anje right now. She's cool, smart and, most importantly, drama-free."

"What?"

"C'mon. That little stunt you just pulled proves my point. Rolling up in here acting like some damn diva. All for what? For you to be the center of attention? This has played out. I'm tired of the head games. I need a girl that's into me as much as I'm into her. Someone who listens and cares about the things I care about."

Tears blur my vision and slide down my face. "I do care about the things—"

"C'mon, Phoenix. Enough with this. Save your acting skills for Hollywood. Frankly, I'm tired of the same old performance."

I step back, seeing the hostility in his eyes. When did he start hating me so much? When did we start drifting apart? More than ever I hate the games I've played with him—all the drama I stirred, thinking it would keep him interested.

"But I love you, Romeo, and you said that you loved me. How can you just walk away from us?"

He shakes his head. "Easy."

I gasp and he finally relents a bit. "Phoenix, you're just hanging on to me because I'm comfortable—because we've been together for so long. If you think about it, we haven't been happy for a long time. We're just together to be the 'it' couple at school."

"That's not true," I say. And it isn't. I've loved him since he passed me that first note in sixth grade asking me to check *yes* or *no* on whether I liked him. I saw us being together through our high school years, attending the same college and then getting married—complete with children and a white picket fence.

"I'm sorry, Phoenix, but it's just over. Let it go." He heads toward me but reaches around for the doorknob.

I'm forced to play my last card. "Romeo, I'm pregnant."

BFF Rule #5
When in doubt, return to rule #1.

chapter 37

Romeo—Teenage Dad

"what the hell did you just say?" I ask, convinced that I heard her wrong.

She takes a deep breath. "I said *I'm pregnant.*"

"By who?"

She rolls her eyes up at me and crosses her arms. "Don't even play that. You know that you're the only one I've ever been with."

"I don't know no such thing. You're always rubbing up and flirting with some damn body."

"That was always just to make you jealous—keep you interested. You are the only person I've ever slept with."

I step away from the door and her. "Naw. Naw," I say. "This is just another one of your games. You're lying."

"I'm not lying, Romeo. I've had morning sickness since school started. It was so bad yesterday that I stayed home. I'm pregnant." She opens the small purse that was resting on her shoulder and hands me some kind of stick.

"What the hell is that?"

"It's a pregnancy test. Read it."

I don't take the stick, but I glance down and see the word *pregnant* on a digital screen. "What? That's supposed to be proof? That just means you got a pregnant girl to piss on that thing. I didn't see you take the test."

She goes back into her purse and removes a slim object wrapped in foil. "Would you like for me to pee on it right now?"

I swallow, but nod my head. This bedroom has an adjoining bathroom. I follow her to it and watch her do the test. Less than three minutes later, I'm looking at a duplicate stick with the word *pregnant* printed on it.

"Oh, shit."

Phoenix flushes the toilet and washes her hands. "Satisfied?"

"Oh, shit," I say again.

"We're going to have a baby," she says, stating the obvious.

"Oh, shit."

"Now do you understand why I came here tonight? We have to get back together. I'm not raising this baby alone."

"Oh, shit."

"Will you please stop saying that?"

"I can't!" I pace the floor and then stop. "We can't have a baby."

"Why the hell not?"

"We're *fifteen!*" I shout.

"That didn't stop us from having sex, now did it?"

"Why weren't you on the pill?"

"Why didn't you use a condom?" she yells back.

My mind draws a blank as I plop down on the corner of the bed. My entire short life flashes before my eyes. "My father is going to kill me when he finds out." And that's if I'm lucky. My father's dreams for me are high, and he doesn't take to disappointment well.

"Don't look like that," Phoenix says. "It's not like we'll be broke and living off welfare. Our parents will help us."

I glance up at her and try to imagine being tied to her for God knows how many years while raising a baby. "I don't know what to do."

Phoenix walks over to the bed and sits down next to me. "The first thing you need to do is break it off with your new girlfriend. *Now.*"

chapter 38

Kierra—I'm Not Ready

"C'MON. I'll lock the door. Nobody is gonna come back here," Chris promises.

I swat at Chris's octopus arms that seem to be everywhere at the same time. "I said *no*." I don't know why I let him talk me into coming back into this room.

"Why are you so scared?" he asks. "I know you've done this before, right?"

I don't answer. What will he think or do if I tell him that I'm a virgin? Will he suddenly lose interest in me? His hands fall onto my jeans and then fumble with the button.

"C'mon. Stop." I finally pull away and flip on the light switch. "There're people right outside the door."

Chris drops his head back and rolls his eyes. "So?"

So?

"Look," I try to reason with him. "I hardly know you."

He chuckles and moves toward me. Before I know it, his arms loop back around my waist, and his hands slip down my ass. "Stop teasin', l'il ma. You know you want to do this." He leans down and nuzzles my ear. It sends a delicious shiver down my spine. "If it's your first time, I promise I'll be gentle."

I close my eyes, not believing how good it feels to be in his arms. Am I really going to do this?

Just then, the DJ outside puts on a slow jam, and before I know it, our bodies begin to sway.

"Have I told you how good you smell?" His lips move from my ear to nip along my jaw. "Hmm?"

Slowly, I shake my head, and then in one magic moment, his lips land on mine. Oh my God, he tastes soo good. The way his tongue moves inside my mouth, I swear I can't think straight.

The kiss deepens. His hands return to the button on my jeans.

Stop him.

I hear a snap and then hear my zipper sliding down.

Stop him.

But I don't stop him, and the next thing I know, he eases me back toward the bed. I enjoy the kissing so maybe the rest won't be so bad. I quickly find out I'm wrong.

There's pain…and then I find myself too embarrassed to tell him to stop. The only good part is that it's over pretty quickly.

"Why are you crying?" he asks.

I didn't even know I *was* crying.

"I didn't do anything wrong," Chris says, jumping up from the bed and pulling up his pants.

"I didn't say you did." I ease up and keep my eyes averted. When I look down, I notice blood on the sheets.

We're both quiet for a moment.

"Then you're all right?"

I nod. "I better just clean up."

"All right. Umm. You want something to drink? I can go get you something."

I'm nodding again and still can't bring myself to look at him.

"Okay, then. I'll be right back." He runs out the door like his shoes are on fire, and to be honest, I don't think he's coming back.

chapter 39

Anjenai—The Beginning of the End

I should have known this was going to happen. Everything was just too perfect. From everyone knowing that *I* am Romeo's new girl to watching him on the football field and then coming to this incredible party. It's been like a dream.

Until *she* showed up. Why can't Phoenix Wilder just let him go? Can't she see that he doesn't love her anymore? I draw a deep breath and try to ignore the open curious gazes of the party crowd. They'd all wanted a fight, and for a few minutes there I was willing to give them one heck of a show. Thank heaven Romeo and Shadiq squashed that bullshit. I'm glad Kierra still has my back. Her and Nicole.

I glance around. "Where did Kierra go?"

"To the cottage," Nicole says. "I saw Chris dragging her in there a few minutes ago."

"Are you all right?" Nicole asks, handing me a cup of punch.

"Yeah. Thanks." I take the cup.

"I would apologize for my sister—well, *half* sister—but what can I say? She's a bitch."

We share a laugh. "Thanks for being there," I tell her. "Couldn't have been easy with you guys being sisters and all."

"It was easier than you think. I'm surprised Tyler didn't pop up."

"Well apparently Kierra wasn't able to convince her to come."

Nicole frowns. "Tyler's here at the party."

I stop drinking, but stare at her over the rim of my cup.

"I was talking to her earlier," Nicole says, glancing around as if she was trying to spot Tyler in the crowd.

I try to act as if she hadn't just planted a new knife in the center of my back. "Oh," is all I can say. I glance at my watch. "It's been fifteen minutes. What the hell are they doing in there?"

"Knowing Phoenix," Nicole says, "she's probably wrapping some kind of new mind game around his head. She's good at that."

That's encouraging. "Maybe I should go in there. You know, to be the voice of reason."

Nicole shrugs.

"You don't think that she could really convince him to go back with her, do you?"

Nicole glances toward the cottage. "Well, they have been together for a long time."

She's right about that. Another five minutes go by, and then I force myself to take action. "Here goes nothing." I stalk toward the cottage. It's not an easy task trying to get from point A to point B with so many people streaming in and out. When I finally make it inside, I'm stunned to see Romeo sitting in one of the high chairs by the breakfast bar with a drink in one hand and Phoenix in the other.

My heart bottoms out. *What the hell?*

I maneuver my way through a throng of people with blood rushing to my head. "What the hell is going on, Romeo?"

He tosses back a shot of something. *He's drinking hard liquor?* I thought he said he didn't like drinking.

"Romeo?" I ask again.

He doesn't look at me. "Yeah?"

Yeah? "What the *hell* are you doing?"

Phoenix turns toward me with a smug smile. "What does it look like? He's enjoying the party with his *real* girlfriend."

People are watching us again.

I stand there, pretty sure I look like a fool. "Romeo, what the hell is she talking about?"

He doesn't answer, but I see his Adam's apple bob up and down.

My sudden rush of tears burn like acid.

"Look," Phoenix says. "It's over. Romeo loves me. You had your fun. Now run along back to the hood and play with your pet rats or whatever the hell it is you poor people do."

"Romeo," I snap. "What is this bitch talking about?" I switch from one foot to the other, feeling my anger boil in my veins. I'm ready to whip both their asses. "What, you're going to let this bitch speak *for* you? You ain't going to man up and tell me the deal?"

Slowly, he turns his head, his eyelids lifting lazily. "I'm sorry."

My head nearly swivels off my neck. "You're sorry? Damn right you're sorry. A sorry piece of shit, if you ask me." I shove his arm hard, and he nearly topples off the stool.

Phoenix jumps her skinny ass in front of me. "Leave him alone. And clean the wax out of your ears. It's OVER!"

"I oughtta…" I launch straight at her ass and grab two handfuls of her blond extensions.

She screams.

Romeo finally comes out his semi-coma and peels me off her. "Anjenai, stop. Let her go. She's pregnant!"

What? He finally extracts me off her, but I fall back into the crowd, lose my footing and somehow hit my head on the edge of a table.

"Oh hell, naw!" To my surprise, Tyler jumps into the mix, swinging at Romeo's head. He goes down, and Phoenix jumps on top of her.

Then Kierra springs from nowhere.

Then Raven.

Then Bianca.

Then Nicole.

And then me.

It feels oddly like old times.

chapter 40

Tyler—Back to Normal

"**HOW** come we're the only ones kicked out of the party and not them?" Kierra asks indignantly, stomping down the estate's curvy driveway. I watch her for a few minutes, thinking that there's something different about her.

"Because we didn't belong there," I say, huffing and rolling my eyes. "We were probably their pet projects for the week," I grumble. "In the end, they stick with their own."

"Well, I'm not all that surprised," Nicole says, flanking my side. "I told you those people were shady as hell."

"Yeah," I say, "but your own sister refused to stick up for you?"

"Well, my *date* did the same thing," Kierra grumbles. "He just walked away like he hadn't spent half the night mopping my neck and…" She never finishes the sentence.

Anjenai says nothing. The pain is evident on her face, and it tugs at my heart.

"Are you all right?" I ask.

Anjenai nods and wipes her eyes, but she hardly looks at me.

For a while, everyone falls silent as our long strides glide us away from our first high school party. When we reach the bottom of the hill at the estate's entrance, we glance around the dark road.

"So what the hell?" Kierra says. "It's late, we're nowhere near a bus stop and I doubt if I have two nickels to rub together. How are we going to get all the way back to Oak Hill?"

"We're going to have to call somebody," I say.

"What—you have physic powers or something?"

Nicole perks up. "I have a cell phone," she suggests.

"Thank you, sweet Jesus," Kierra says and waits for Nicole to hand it over. "Now who are we going to call? My sister is working, and she'll tell us to hoof it."

Nicole bites her lip. "My dad will pick me up, but I don't how he'll feel about driving you guys back to Oak Hill. He tends to avoid that side of town." She shrugs. "Sorry."

We roll our eyes at that nonsense.

"My granny is out of the question," Anjenai says. "Even if her legs were feeling up to it, she would have to bring my four brothers, and all of us can't fit into the car, too."

I sigh. "I guess that leaves my father."

"You think he'll come?" Kierra asks.

"I guess there's only one way to find out." I take the phone and dial home. My father picks up on the second ring. "Hello, Dad? I need your help."

chapter 41

The BFFs—Together Again

Tyler's dad arrives at the estate twenty minutes later, looking mad as hell. "What the hell happened?" he asks jumping out the car to check the girls over. "Did some boy do something to you?"

"No, Dad. We just need a ride home," Tyler says, getting in the backseat of the car.

Her father doesn't let the matter drop. "I'm driving up to that party," he announces.

"No!" the girls shout at him.

"We've made big enough fools of ourselves," Tyler informs him. "Can we *please* just go home?"

He stares at them as they pile into the backseat.

"And can we drop off our friend Nicole? She's staying not too far from here." Tyler shuts the door, and they all wait for Mr. Jamison to climb back into the driver's seat. When he does, he looks back at them in the rearview mirror and meets his daughter's gaze. "We're going to talk about this when we get home."

Tyler folds her arms and looks away.

Anjenai is still sniffing silently to herself.

"Hey," Tyler says. "I'm sorry about what happened back there."

Anjenai gives a half laugh. "No, you're not. You didn't want me to be with him any more than Phoenix did."

That was true.

Anjenai wipes another tear from her eye. "But I appreciate you jumping in when you did. It means a lot."

Tyler lowers her gaze. "I know I've been a lousy friend lately," she whispers. "I'm truly sorry about trippin' like that. But it just took seeing Romeo push you into the crowd like that for me to snap out of it. I was being a bitch."

"Yeah." Anjenai finally looks at Tyler and knows that a lifetime of friendship is on the line. "But I always knew that."

They laugh, but then slowly sober up.

"I love you, Anje. You're my best friend."

Anje smiles. "I love you, too. You're still my girl...and I'm sorry about what I said. You know...about—"

"Forget it. We both said some things we didn't mean."

With that, Anje threw her arms around Tyler. And for the first time in a long time, Tyler didn't mind being touched.

"Does this mean we're all friends again?" Kierra asks.

Tyler pulls back. "Damn right we are." She reaches into her jeans pocket and pulls out the broken B gold chain. "I believe this belongs to you."

Anje smiles and takes the chain back. "Thanks. The BFFs are back together again."

They turn and look at Nicole. "All four of us."

Nicole beams. "You mean it?"

They nod. "Absolutely."

"Thanks, girls." They give each other a group hug in the back of the car.

Leon looks back at them through the rearview mirror and smiles.

When they pull away, Anje voices her fears. "You know it's going to be hell when we go back to school Monday."

"Yeah, maybe," Tyler says. "But I think we can handle anything that comes our way."

Kierra turns and looks out the side window. "I hope you're right."

* * * * *

Stay tuned for Book 2 in the BFFs series

Discussion Questions for *Chasing Romeo*

Anjenai, Kierra and Tyler have been best friends since they were babies. How important is it to you to have friends you depend on to stick by you through thick and thin?

From the moment the BFFs enter Maynard Jackson High, they learn the hierarchy of the Haves and Have Nots. Does your school suffer from the same social politics? If so how do you deal with it?

The Red Bones represent a unique problem in African-American culture: the belief that lighter skin blacks are better than darker skin blacks. How do you feel about this issue? Do you see this situation playing out in your own life, your school or your neighborhood?

For the first time in their lives, the BFFs are confronted with the problem of liking the same guy. Has a boy ever come between you and your friends? If so, how did you deal with it? Did it damage the relationship?

Despite agreeing that none of them would pursue Romeo, Anjenai followed her heart. Was she wrong to do so? Did she deserve what happened in the end?

Kierra likes to pretend that nothing ever gets to her. But in truth, her home life is in total disarray. Is it common for teens to hide their home life if they come from a dysfunctional family?

Tyler has an explosive temper. She reacts before thinking. Have you ever dealt with someone with anger issues? Do you think her friends are helping or hurting her by always letting her pop off?

Nicole desperately wants to belong and suffers from an eating disorder. Eating is a very common way to deal with emotions like stress and peer pressure. What are some better ways to deal with those feelings?

Sometimes life sucks…

JADED

An INDIGO Novel

Essence bestselling author

Monica McKayhan

Jade Morgan wants her parents to get back together.
Instead, her dad proposes to his new girlfriend—who
has the nerve to ask Jade to be a bridesmaid. Jade's new
boyfriend, Terrence, thinks Jade should give her future
stepmother a chance. And as if things could get even
worse, Jade thinks Terrence is hiding something. She's
feeling jaded about life, all right…this is *so* not how it was
supposed to be.

*Coming the first week of December
wherever books are sold.*